I0819837

OVERLOOK CATERING SERVICE
SECURITY
0001740
FOG
MACHIN
STEPHEN
KING
GLENN
CHADBOURNE

WELCOME MY FRIENDS To The SHOW THAT NEVER ENDS!

Stephen King has had more movie, television, options and productions than any other living author. If you're reading this then you're a Stephen King fan and his story visuals are part of what makes his writing so attractive; the "mind movie" he delivers for his Constant Readers. Films are just the icing on the story cake! However it's always fun to see what these cinematic creative teams come up with. Certainly there have been wild imaginings, but there are also films that are pure magic on the big screen. One has even become the favorite movie of all time as of this writing. *The Shawshank Redemption* is at No. 1 at IMDB.com.

That look on folks faces when I tell them *Shawshank* is based on a Stephen King story... Priceless.

Before all the current frenzy of Hollywood activity it began with a short novel in the early '70's that Stephen King considered a failure, and threw in the trash: *Carrie*. His wife, Tabitha, pulled it out and told him it was good. Very good. Screenwriter, Lawrence D. Cohen, also recognized the greatness of the story early on when it was sitting in a pile at his boss's office that produced films. Cohen has a life long history, over forty-five years, of working on *Carrie* in film, Broadway shows, and TV versions, all over the world! And *Carrie*, with director Brian DePalma, was just the start of the King motion picture cavalcade. Then came Stanley Kubrick's version of *The Shining*, the Romero / King collaboration of *Creepshow*, David Cronenberg's *The Dead Zone*, John Carpenter's *Christine*, Rob Reiner's *Stand By Me* and *Misery*, Mick Garris's *Sleepwalkers*, *Riding the Bullet*. Frank Darabont's *The Shawshank Redemption*, *The Green Mile* and *The Mist*. Mark Pavia's *The Night Flier*, Scott Hick's *Hearts in Atlantis*, Taylor Hackford's *Dolores Claiborne*, and more recently, Mike Flanigan's *Doctor Sleep*, and Andy Muschietti's 2017 *IT*. This new version of *IT* became the highest grossing box office film of all time! *IT* was massive and released as two films, two years apart, grossing over 1.4 billion worldwide. These directors (and I'm not able to include everyone) is a who's who of insightful and creative filmmakers that have brought a bevy of King's work to the big screen. These films remind us all that along with a great story teller, there is also some great talents bringing us his vision on screen. We all benefit from seeing more Stephen King in their unique visions. We have a lot to look forward to in the coming years.

This *2021 Stephen King Catalog Desk Calendar* you hold in your hands only covers the theatrical releases of this author's work. However there are a couple of recent exceptions as I've included a few streaming and network original productions. I feel they're more theatrical quality and deserve to be included here. From fun facts, quotes, and trivia that will reinvigorate your knowledge of these visual feasts, and hopefully bring you new information. We hope you'll have fun with what we've brought to this years screening. For me this has been so much fun revisiting these films with this calendar. We began last years 2020 calendar with *The Stand* theme (still available from us and at Amazon.com – all over the world!), and we have a lot more in store for calendars in the years to come.

With all the information we've gleaned for you within, I just want you to be aware that this calendar is *full* of spoilers. I've tried to keep it fun and interesting without trying to give much away. Some of these films have been around for over four decades, but a lot of you have seen them. I'm sure there will be films in here you haven't seen, but just keep this in mind when you're reading, spoilers ahead!

So pop some corn and pop in a King flick we've highlighted within because... *it's showtime!*

Kill the lights!

– Dave Hinchberger

STEPHEN KING GOES TO THE MOVIES!

THE STEPHEN KING CATALOG 2021 DESK CALENDAR

Edited by
Dave Hinchberger

Artwork by
Glenn Chadbourne

DECEMBER

28 MONDAY

29 TUESDAY

30 WEDNESDAY

STORYBOARDING

"I usually only storyboard action and FX sequences, because they need to be very specific. Amazingly we followed these almost exactly."

– Mick Garris,
Director, *Riding the Bullet.*

An actual storyboarding sequence that was used in *Riding the Bullet*. Continued on the next page.

JANUARY

31 THURSDAY

New Year's Eve

1 FRIDAY

New Year's Day

2 SATURDAY

3 SUNDAY

GETTING GRAPHIC

A storyboard is a graphic organizer that consists of illustrations and images displayed in sequence for the purpose of pre-visualising a motion picture, animation, motion graphic or interactive media sequence. I was on the set of Stephen King's *The Mist* and right there within the grocery store you see in the film was a large 4′ x 8′ board with a layout of illustrations of the filming being produced that day. It's a fascinating process and helps keep the ideas visually in mind when working on a scene. This storyboarding process originally began at Walt Disney Productions during the early 1930s.

JANUARY

4 MONDAY

5 TUESDAY

6 WEDNESDAY

IN NAME ONLY

The Lawnmower Man film became quite the controversy when it was released. Stephen King legally had his name removed from the production. The original story, by King, features a man who's hired to cut grass that eventually becomes a demon that is literally eating grass, and *anything* in it's path. However the film bore no resemblance to the original story and the author felt this was a betrayal to him and his audience. I mention the film and story here as even though King had his name removed, it will always have some association with him in film history, I post about it here to educate. With that said you can view a correct *graphic* release of this story that was originally

JANUARY

7 THURSDAY

8 FRIDAY

9 SATURDAY

10 SUNDAY

published in a 1981 Marvel publication, in *Bizarre Adventures #29.* That issue has been long out of print but fortunately a portfolio of this issue, in it's complete story format, was released in a beautiful set in 2014. This is the only the second time it has ever been released that represents King's true story. This portfolio is in stock and available at StephenKingCatalog.com

The Lawnmower Man Artist Portfolio Edition, 2014, by Walter Simonsson and IDW.

Available at StephenKingCatalog.com

DECEMBER

S	M	T	W	T	F	S
		1	2	3	4	5
6	7	8	9	10	11	12
13	14	15	16	17	18	19
20	21	22	23	24	25	26
27	28	29	30	31		

JANUARY

S	M	T	W	T	F	S
					1	2
3	4	5	6	7	8	9
10	11	12	13	14	15	16
17	18	19	20	21	22	23
24	25	26	27	28	29	30
31						

FEBRUARY

S	M	T	W	T	F	S
	1	2	3	4	5	6
7	8	9	10	11	12	13
14	15	16	17	18	19	20
21	22	23	24	25	26	27
28						

JANUARY

11 MONDAY

12 TUESDAY

13 WEDNESDAY

What is the exact name of the plane that the *Night Flier* pilots across the country in this story? What color is it?

Answers:

1. Cessna Skymaster 337. This was also known as the Cessna Super Skymaster for a short time. 2. Black (black as night, if you will…)

JANUARY

14 THURSDAY

15 FRIDAY

16 SATURDAY

17 SUNDAY

"Never believe what you publish, never publish what you believe."

– Richard Dees, *The Night Flier*

DECEMBER

S	M	T	W	T	F	S
		1	2	3	4	5
6	7	8	9	10	11	12
13	14	15	16	17	18	19
20	21	22	23	24	25	26
27	28	29	30	31		

JANUARY

S	M	T	W	T	F	S
					1	2
3	4	5	6	7	8	9
10	11	12	13	14	15	16
17	18	19	20	21	22	23
24	25	26	27	28	29	30
31						

FEBRUARY

S	M	T	W	T	F	S
	1	2	3	4	5	6
7	8	9	10	11	12	13
14	15	16	17	18	19	20
21	22	23	24	25	26	27
28						

JANUARY

18 MONDAY

Martin Luther King, Jr. Day

19 TUESDAY

20 WEDNESDAY

Inauguration Day

SHINING INSPIRATION.

Stephen King, and producer Mark Carliner were in the midst of making the Mick Garris TV series of Stephen King's *The Shining* in Colorado. They frequented a local video store during this production and discovered a movie called *Riget* (Kingdom in English). They were so entranced with this film they tried to buy the rights to this Danish original. Unfortunately for them Columbia Pictures had already acquired these rights for a future production. Five years later Columbia decided it was never going to come to fruition and sold the rights to Stephen King and company in exchange for his novella, *Secret Window, Secret Garden*. Which of course became the film starring Johnny Depp, *Secret Window. Riget* became the TV series, *Kingdom Hospital*, that Stephen King wrote for and produced. Funny how Hollywood works and not only one, but two, King productions were born… which all started in a Colorado video store.

JANUARY

21 THURSDAY

22 FRIDAY

23 SATURDAY

24 SUNDAY

LET MORTON REIGN.

Johnny Depp's character, the author Morton Rainey, is living at his cabin on a lake in the film, *Secret Window*. Toward the end of the movie, this character purchases items at the grocer's. One of the items is a box of *Morton's* Salt. Morton's motto is "When it RAINS, it pours." Thus… Morton Rainey.

DECEMBER

S	M	T	W	T	F	S
		1	2	3	4	5
6	7	8	9	10	11	12
13	14	15	16	17	18	19
20	21	22	23	24	25	26
27	28	29	30	31		

JANUARY

S	M	T	W	T	F	S
					1	2
3	4	5	6	7	8	9
10	11	12	13	14	15	16
17	18	19	20	21	22	23
24	25	26	27	28	29	30
31						

FEBRUARY

S	M	T	W	T	F	S
	1	2	3	4	5	6
7	8	9	10	11	12	13
14	15	16	17	18	19	20
21	22	23	24	25	26	27
28						

JANUARY

25 MONDAY | **26** TUESDAY | **27** WEDNESDAY

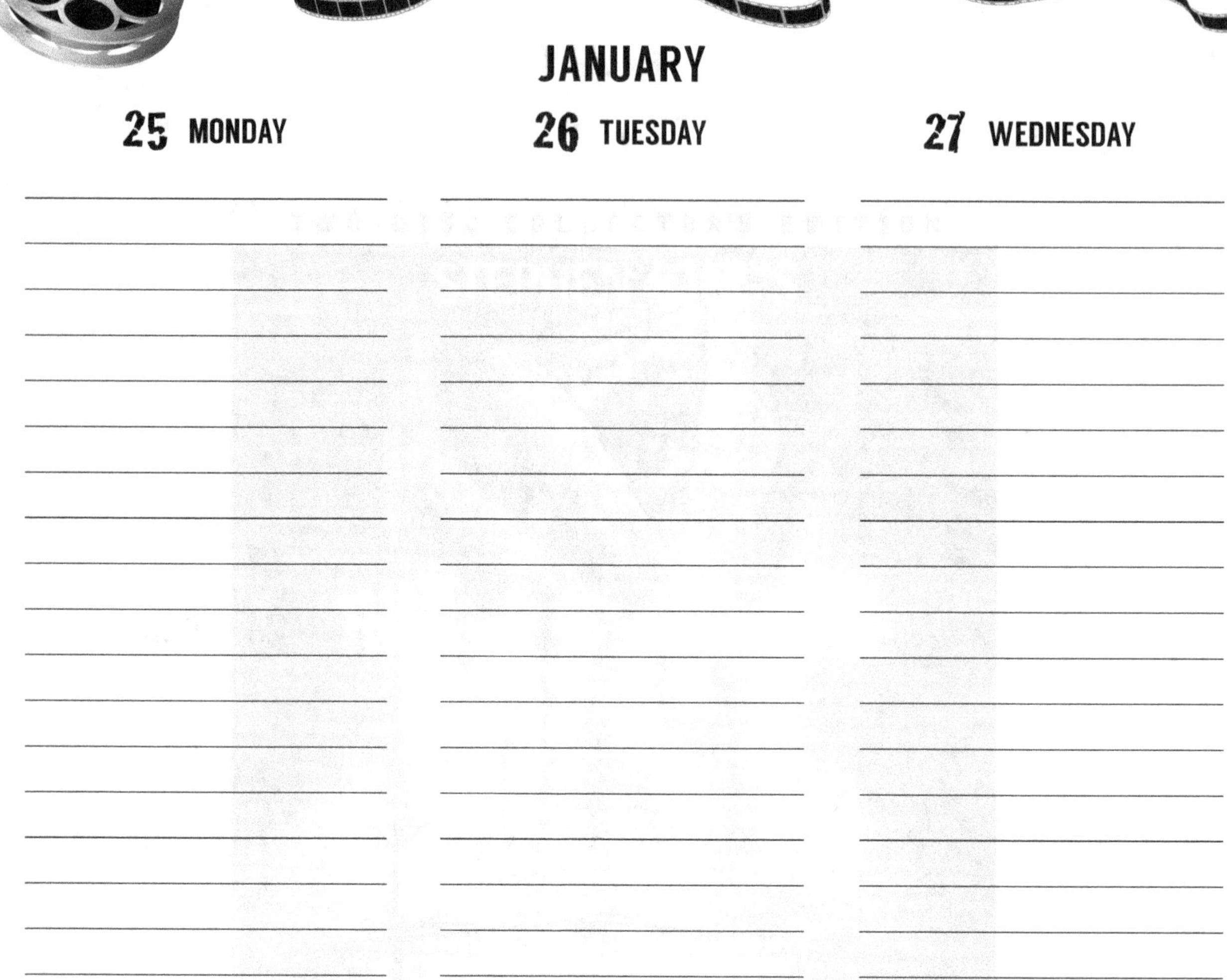

BACK IN BLACK...AND WHITE!

The Mist Director, Frank Darabont, who worked on bringing this film to movie screens for twenty years, originally wanted to release *The Mist* in black and white. He said in his introduction to the black and white version on the 2 disc Blu-Ray (2008), "I've always had it in mind to shoot *The Mist* in black and white." and mentioned that this idea was inspired by such iconic films as George Romero's *Night of the Living Dead* (1968) and the "pre-color" work of Ray Harryhausen. While the film's theatrical release was in color, the director has described the black and white print as his "preferred version," his "director's cut, for fellow film buff's and geeks who really dig black and white movies, this would be the version to watch." Now you can watch both versions of *The Mist*, thanks to Frank Darabont and his team who made it happen. This alternate version really does enhance the experience for anyone who appreciates an earlier, horror, black and white era. As film fans, we're fortunate Darabont went the extra mile. The 2-disc Blu-ray release contains Darabont's black and white, and color, versions, along with extras including a sit down interview with Stephen King and Frank Darabont.
(available at StephenKingCatalog.com)

JANUARY

28 THURSDAY

29 FRIDAY

30 SATURDAY

31 SUNDAY

"The story is less about the monsters outside than about the monsters inside, the people you're stuck with, your friends and neighbors breaking under the strain."

– Frank Darabont, *The Mist* Director.

Screen capture of the black and white version of *The Mist* showing an example of what you can expect from the 2 disc Blu-Ray that includes this version.

DECEMBER

S	M	T	W	T	F	S
		1	2	3	4	5
6	7	8	9	10	11	12
13	14	15	16	17	18	19
20	21	22	23	24	25	26
27	28	29	30	31		

JANUARY

S	M	T	W	T	F	S
					1	2
3	4	5	6	7	8	9
10	11	12	13	14	15	16
17	18	19	20	21	22	23
24	25	26	27	28	29	30
31						

FEBRUARY

S	M	T	W	T	F	S
	1	2	3	4	5	6
7	8	9	10	11	12	13
14	15	16	17	18	19	20
21	22	23	24	25	26	27
28						

FEBRUARY

1 MONDAY

2 TUESDAY

The Night Flier – Released Theatrically 2-2-1998. It was initialy released thru cable TV on HBO on 11-7-1997.

Groundhog Day

3 WEDNESDAY

The Night Flier Japanese poster / video release artwork, 1997.

AN INSIDE VIEW

1. What is the name of the tabloid in the film, *The Night Flier*?
2. Richard Dees, the protaganist in *The Night Flier*, made a previous appearance in what Stephen King novel?

FEBRUARY

4 THURSDAY

5 FRIDAY

6 SATURDAY

7 SUNDAY

Answers:

1. *Inside View.*
2. *The Dead Zone.* Richard Dees offers Johnny Smith a job as a psychic for his tabloid paper, *Inside View.* He was turned down. Physically.

JANUARY

S	M	T	W	T	F	S
					1	2
3	4	5	6	7	8	9
10	11	12	13	14	15	16
17	18	19	20	21	22	23
24	25	26	27	28	29	30
31						

FEBRUARY

S	M	T	W	T	F	S
	1	2	3	4	5	6
7	8	9	10	11	12	13
14	15	16	17	18	19	20
21	22	23	24	25	26	27
28						

MARCH

S	M	T	W	T	F	S
	1	2	3	4	5	6
7	8	9	10	11	12	13
14	15	16	17	18	19	20
21	22	23	24	25	26	27
28	29	30	31			

FEBRUARY

8 MONDAY

9 TUESDAY

10 WEDNESDAY

THE ROCK

Stephen King used the name Castle Rock from the fictional mountain fort in William Golding's 1954 novel *Lord of the Flies*. The town first appeared in King's novel *The Dead Zone*, then in *Cujo*. His novellas, "The Body" and "Rita Hayworth and the Shawshank Redemption," also have both stories take place in Castle Rock. The town makes an explosive appearance in the novel, *Needful Things* in which Stephen King touted it was to be the last Castle Rock story. However it's made several appearances in short stories and novels since then. Director and film associate of Stephen King's, George Romero, has stated that the first appearance in a film of the words Castle Rock was the directional street post sign in *Creepshow* at the end of the segment "The Lonesome Death of Jordy Verrill." This aged and ragged wood sign is at a crossroads and shows you the direction and miles to Portland, Boston, and Castle Rock.

Rob Reiner's production company was named Castle

FEBRUARY

11 THURSDAY

12 FRIDAY

Chinese New Year

13 SATURDAY

14 SUNDAY

Valentine's Day

Rock Entertainment after the success of *Stand By Me*, based on King's *The Body*. Castle Rock Entertainment went on to make, or distribute, many more Stephen King films, These include the Stephen King titles, *Dolores Claiborne*, *Needful Things*, *Misery*, *The Shawshank Redemption*, *The Green Mile*, *Hearts in Atlantis*, and *Dreamcatcher*. as well as the TV series, *Castle Rock*, that spawned two seasons as of this writing. However that version of "The Rock" is a story for another time, and another calendar.

JANUARY

S	M	T	W	T	F	S
					1	2
3	4	5	6	7	8	9
10	11	12	13	14	15	16
17	18	19	20	21	22	23
24	25	26	27	28	29	30
31						

FEBRUARY

S	M	T	W	T	F	S
	1	2	3	4	5	6
7	8	9	10	11	12	13
14	15	16	17	18	19	20
21	22	23	24	25	26	27
28						

MARCH

S	M	T	W	T	F	S
	1	2	3	4	5	6
7	8	9	10	11	12	13
14	15	16	17	18	19	20
21	22	23	24	25	26	27
28	29	30	31			

FEBRUARY

15 MONDAY	16 TUESDAY	17 WEDNESDAY
President's Day	Mardi Gras	

BIG DRIVER was released on the Lifetime network, making this a TV movie. However I've included it here with motion picture releases of King's work because it was given the motion picture treatment. This isn't like any TV movie I've ever experienced on this channel. Between a tight script, which Richard Christian Matheson excels in, and the quality of the acting, makes this a couple of steps above the TV norm.

LIFE & DEATH ON THE ROAD. Joan Jett, the rock n' roll singer / songwriter / performer appears in *Big Driver.* What is the hit song she is most associated with? This is the second film with actress Maria Bello in a Stephen King production. What is the first Stephen King film she acted in? The screenplay adaptation for *Big Driver* was written by author Richard Christian Matheson. Mr. Matheson also wrote one other Stephen King adaptation. What is it?

FEBRUARY

18 THURSDAY

19 FRIDAY

20 SATURDAY

21 SUNDAY

Answers:

1. "I Love Rock n' Roll."
2. *Secret Window* with Johnny Depp.
3. "Battleground," a short story that appeared in Stephen King's first collection, *Night Shift*. Matheson also adapted the short story which was made into an iconic episode of the TNT series *Nightmares and Dreamscapes* and won two Emmys.

JANUARY

S	M	T	W	T	F	S
					1	2
3	4	5	6	7	8	9
10	11	12	13	14	15	16
17	18	19	20	21	22	23
24	25	26	27	28	29	30
31						

FEBRUARY

S	M	T	W	T	F	S
	1	2	3	4	5	6
7	8	9	10	11	12	13
14	15	16	17	18	19	20
21	22	23	24	25	26	27
28						

MARCH

S	M	T	W	T	F	S
	1	2	3	4	5	6
7	8	9	10	11	12	13
14	15	16	17	18	19	20
21	22	23	24	25	26	27
28	29	30	31			

Japanese DVD, 2015

FEBRUARY

22 MONDAY

23 TUESDAY

24 WEDNESDAY

DIGGING SHAWSHANK.

1. What is the original title of the novella that *The Shawshank Redemption* is based on by Stephen King and what is the name of the collection where it originally appeared in print?
2. There is a poster of a beautiful movie starlet from the 1940's that hangs in Andy Defrusne's cell and is pivital to the film's story. Who is this actress?
3. The photograph of this actress was taken for which magazine and when was it published?
4. *The Shawshank Redemption* was nominated for seven Academy Awards. How many did this deserving film win?

FEBRUARY

25 THURSDAY

26 FRIDAY

27 SATURDAY

28 SUNDAY

2019 German DVD release. Die Verurteilten translates to *The Condemned*.

Answers:

1. *Rita Hayworth and The Shawshank Redemption* originally appeared in the 1982 collection, *Different Seasons*.
2. Rita Hayworth.
3. The photo was taken by Bob Landry for Life magazine August 11, 1941 issue. Rita Hayworth graced the cover of that issue as well as a featured photo spread within of her, also by Landry. She was considered the most popular pinup girl during the World War II era.
4. None. The irony here is that *The Shawshank Redemption* has been listed as the number one movie on the IMDB list with a rating of 9.2 / 10 for years. *The Godfather* is No. 2 with 9.1. Who needs an Oscar when you've got the people keeping you at the top?

MARCH

1 MONDAY

2 TUESDAY

3 WEDNESDAY

The Mangler – Released 3-3-1995

The Lawnmower Man – Released 3-3-1992

MANGLED, IN NAME ONLY.

Voice actor, Jim Cummings, discussed during the 2018 Fan Expo Canada in Toronto his many voice roles (over 500 by 2020) he's performed over the decades. He's voiced everything from TV and film animation to video games. Voicing roles with *Star Trek*, *Frankenstein* in *Scooby Doo*, *Tales From the Crypt*, *Winnie the Pooh*, and too many Disney films to mention here. Cummings said during the Expo that one role he took on was where "he voiced a haunted dry cleaning press." Cummings said he was happy to see his name misspelled as "Tim Cummings" when the film was released. We can only assume this is in reference to the fact that it was a critical and commercial flop. All these years later it has a small cult following with the b-movie crowd, and was released in 2018 Blu-Ray 4K remastered and uncut version. I guess they scooped up some of the guts from the cutting room floor... and tucked them back in.

MARCH

4 THURSDAY

5 FRIDAY

6 SATURDAY

7 SUNDAY

HOOPER ENGLUND

1. **Director Tobe Hooper directed an earlier Stephen King adaptation. What is it?**
2. **One of the main actors in *The Mangler* is known for playing an infamous horror character in the movie series *A Nightmare on Elm Street*. Who is the actor and what character did he play?**

Answers:

1. Tobe Hooper directed the 1979 TV mini-series, *Salem's Lot*, Stephen King's second novel. It received much acclaim when it originally aired, and scared a few viewers watching at home too. I imagine a lot of blankets over the head, and popcorn spilled those nights. Many claimed to make sure their windows were locked before they went to bed. The series still maintains a popular approval from fans, now, over forty years later.
2. Robert Englund portrayed the hand razored madman, Freddy Krueger in the *Nightmare on Elm Street* related films.

MARCH

8 MONDAY

9 TUESDAY

Children of the Corn
– Released 3-9-1984

10 WEDNESDAY

As Burt and Vicki are driving in the beginning of the film there's a copy of a book on the dashboard.

1. **What is the title of this book and who is the author?**
2. **Why is this book important to the film, *Children of the Corn*?**
3. **What magazine did the original appearance of *Children of the Corn* appear in?**

MARCH

11 THURSDAY

12 FRIDAY

New Year's Day

13 SATURDAY

14 SUNDAY

Daylight Savings Begins

Answers:

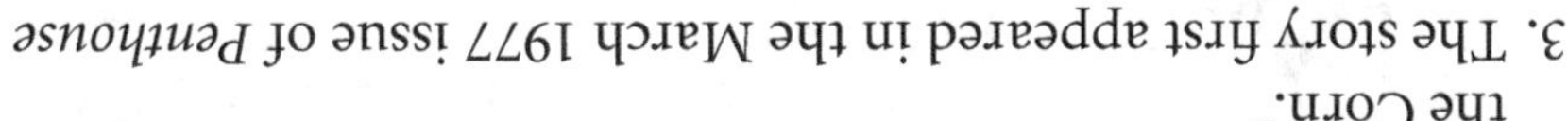

1. *Night Shift* by Stephen King
2. This is the short story collection that featured the story, "Children of the Corn."
3. The story first appeared in the March 1977 issue of *Penthouse* magazine.

FEBRUARY

S	M	T	W	T	F	S
	1	2	3	4	5	6
7	8	9	10	11	12	13
14	15	16	17	18	19	20
21	22	23	24	25	26	27
28						

MARCH

S	M	T	W	T	F	S
	1	2	3	4	5	6
7	8	9	10	11	12	13
14	15	16	17	18	19	20
21	22	23	24	25	26	27
28	29	30	31			

APRIL

S	M	T	W	T	F	S
				1	2	3
4	5	6	7	8	9	10
11	12	13	14	15	16	17
18	19	20	21	22	23	24
25	26	27	28	29	30	

MARCH

15 MONDAY

16 TUESDAY

17 WEDNESDAY

St. Patrick's Day

William Goldman, the screenwriter of excellent films such as *The Marathon Man*, *Butch Cassidy and the Sundance Kid* (he won the Academy Award for this one), and my personal favorite, *The Princess Bride*, is the screenwriter of *Dreamcatcher* and two other Stephen King novels. Speaking of horror, Goldman is also the novelist / screenwriter of the story *No Way to Treat a Lady* (another personal favorite), starring Rod Stieger. This material deals with murder, rape, and takes you down a deft tunnel of psychotic madness. Definitely a horror tale. He wrote that story under the pseudonym Harry Longbaugh, which is the real name of The Sundance Kid. Interesting tie in with horror, and a great writer to work on King adaptations. What are the other two screenplays that he wrote?

MARCH

18 THURSDAY

19 FRIDAY

20 SATURDAY

21 SUNDAY

Dreamcatcher
– Released 3-21-2003

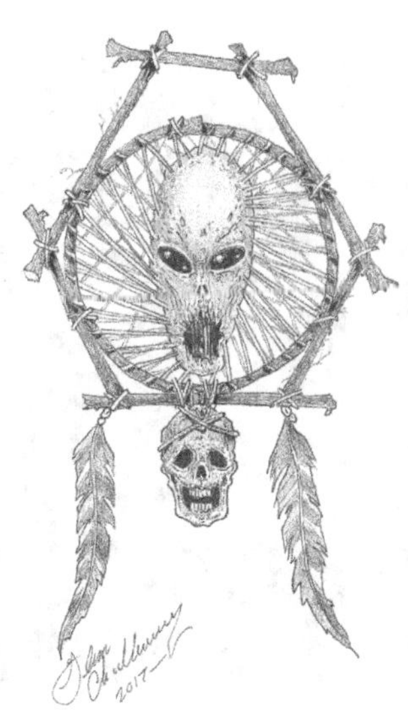

Answer:

The three films that William Goldman based on Stephen King novels are: 1. *Dreamcatcher*, 2. *Misery* and 3. *Hearts in Atlantis*.

FEBRUARY

S	M	T	W	T	F	S
	1	2	3	4	5	6
7	8	9	10	11	12	13
14	15	16	17	18	19	20
21	22	23	24	25	26	27
28						

MARCH

S	M	T	W	T	F	S
	1	2	3	4	5	6
7	8	9	10	11	12	13
14	15	16	17	18	19	20
21	22	23	24	25	26	27
28	29	30	31			

APRIL

S	M	T	W	T	F	S
				1	2	3
4	5	6	7	8	9	10
11	12	13	14	15	16	17
18	19	20	21	22	23	24
25	26	27	28	29	30	

MARCH

22 MONDAY

23 TUESDAY

24 WEDNESDAY

Dolores Claiborne
– Released 3-24-1995

Dolores Claiborne, Spanish DVD, 2000 Warner Bros.

DID YOU KNOW?

Kathy Bates stated in an interview about her acting career that her performance as Dolores Claiborne was her favorite performance she had ever given[1]. During the fight scene between Joe and Dolores Claiborne, Dolores threatens Joe with a stay in Shawshank prison. Shawshank prison is the primary setting for *The Shawshank Redemption* (1994), which was also based on a story by Stephen King. Tony Gilroy, who created an insightful and emotional screenplay for *Dolores Claiborne*, went on to write many popular and successful films. Most notably he wrote *Rogue One: A Star Wars Story*. He also wrote, the *Jason Bourne* trilogy of films starring Matt Damon. He then wrote the screenplay and directed *The Bourne Legacy*. He adapted *Armageddon*, the Michael Bay action film. I'd say Dolores gave those films, and Tony Gilroy, a helluva good footing to begin with back in 1995.

MARCH

25 THURSDAY

26 FRIDAY

27 SATURDAY

28 SUNDAY

What is the town that is closest to Little Tall Island in Maine?

Answer:

Derry. However this isn't a real town, and you won't find Little Tall Island or Derry on any map of Maine. Except in the mind, and stories, of Stephen King's world. Taylor Hackford, the director of *Dolores Claiborne*, had his team go and scout these areas for possible filming locations. They came back to him and informed him there wasn't any towns with those names in Maine. Hackford assumed since the book of *Dolores Claiborne* had a map within it that the area was a real location in Maine. His film team ended up filming the areas of Nova Scotia, Canada. Notably in Lunenburg, Mahone Bay, and Chester, to make up Little Tall Island. There was also a major storm once in Little Tall Island, but that's a tale for another time…

MARCH

29 MONDAY

30 TUESDAY

31 WEDNESDAY

BACK FROM THE DEAD. . . AGAIN.

The 2019 adaptation of *Pet Sematary* had Stephen King fans excited for the possibilities of actually bringing the scare that the novel originally gave us back on its release, November 14th, 1983. The story deserved a cinematic remake after the 1989 version, although gory fun on it's own terms, I never felt it was up to speed when it came to bringing the novels story to the big screen. You see *Pet Sematary*, Stephen King's vision, scared the hell out of me. The story is as evil as they come, and it disturbed me. It probably hit me harder than some as I had two young sons at the time. So when the Mary Lambert directed version was released it wasn't what I was expecting, and yes it had it's moments, but I was disappointed. Possibly it was the timing of when it was released and the world just wasn't ready for that kind of shock, that onscreen evil. Hey, they had to fill theater seats, but the story suffered for it. The novel story is dark. It's dark I tell ya, at least for that time. The world has changed and there are more authors, and even more books, that deal with pretty bleak material in the horror genre out there. However King's novel of insidious darkness, with a wholesome family

APRIL

1 THURSDAY

2 FRIDAY

3 SATURDAY

4 SUNDAY

Easter

moving close to evil ground, was brought to the masses and it had us squirming in our seats back then. That brings us back to *Pet Sematary*, the 2019 version. A group of us get together when King films are released and we make an afternoon of it at a theater in downtown Atlanta. Of course we were all curious about this new vision and set a date. After these gatherings we sit around and discuss the films. The consensus? It was... "okay," "not bad," "had a few scares," and a few of us "liked it." It was closer to the original novels vision, it's dark in theme, and its simply a dark looking film. Overall it gave me a chill here and there, it does have it's horror charms to draw you in and pounce, literally. I liked it. Was it the story I was expecting? Well, not exactly. I think the filming / editing of the time line could have been better. It actually did well at the box office, and these days most King films do. It still isn't the novel. Not many are, but some get close. I haven't read it since 1983. After all this time, I should. I find that I'm mostly callous to evil doings these days, well, at least in fiction/film anyway. Would *Pet Sematary*, the novel, still hold some disturbing sway over me? I think it's time to find out. – Dave Hinchberger

Pet Seminary, 2019 UK Movie Poster Art.

MARCH

S	M	T	W	T	F	S
	1	2	3	4	5	6
7	8	9	10	11	12	13
14	15	16	17	18	19	20
21	22	23	24	25	26	27
28	29	30	31			

APRIL

S	M	T	W	T	F	S
				1	2	3
4	5	6	7	8	9	10
11	12	13	14	15	16	17
18	19	20	21	22	23	24
25	26	27	28	29	30	

MAY

S	M	T	W	T	F	S
						1
2	3	4	5	6	7	8
9	10	11	12	13	14	15
16	17	18	19	20	21	22
23	24	25	26	27	28	29
30	31					

APRIL

5 MONDAY

Pet Sematary (2019)
– Released 4-5-2019

6 TUESDAY

7 WEDNESDAY

WHO IS... THIS?

There are some special guests that made cameos in *Sleepwalkers*. Can you name these iconic guests? There is one cameo who launched into a space opera for decades!

Answers:

Stephen King as the graveyard caretaker. Director John Landis (*Animal House*, *The Blues Brothers*) as a Lab Technician. Author, director, and painter, Clive Barker (*The Hellbound Heart* film series, *Books of Blood*) as the Forensic Technician. Director Joe Dante (*Gremlins*, *The Howling*) as a Lab Assistant. Tobe Hooper (*'Salem's Lot*, *Poltergeist*). Mark Hamill, who played Luke Skywalker in *Star Wars*, is in the very first scene in the film. He plays a policeman. Director Mick Garris got to know Mark Hamill when he used to see him daily when Garris worked at Lucasfilm.

APRIL

1 THURSDAY

2 FRIDAY

3 SATURDAY

4 SUNDAY

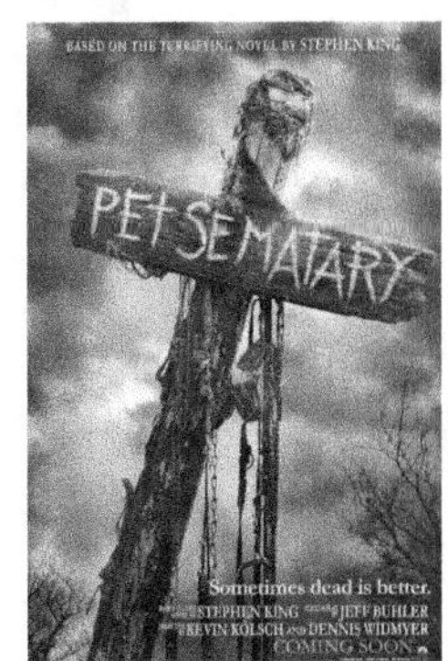

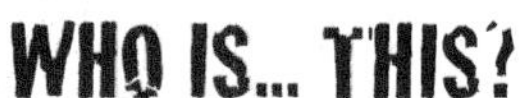

APRIL

8 THURSDAY

9 FRIDAY

10 SATURDAY

Sleepwalkers
– Released 4-10-1992

11 SUNDAY

WALK N' ROLL!

What 45 single record is playing on the turntable at the beginning of *Sleepwalkers*? This music is also featured in the trailer for *Sleepwalkers*.

Answer:

"Sleep Walk" by Santo & Johnny. Released June, 1959. They are known best for this instrumental melody "Sleep Walk", one of the biggest hits of the golden age of rock 'n' roll, which became a regional success in Brooklyn, New York, and eventually scored the top of the Billboard pop chart at #1 for two weeks when it was released nationally during 1959. They wrote it at 2 A.M. as one brother had an idea for a song, woke up the other brother and appropriately named it "Sleep Walk." After other recordings and films, it eventually became the theme song for this Stephen King original film. Which in turn was the inspiration for this original story / screenplay.

MARCH

S	M	T	W	T	F	S
	1	2	3	4	5	6
7	8	9	10	11	12	13
14	15	16	17	18	19	20
21	22	23	24	25	26	27
28	29	30	31			

APRIL

S	M	T	W	T	F	S
				1	2	3
4	5	6	7	8	9	10
11	12	13	14	15	16	17
18	19	20	21	22	23	24
25	26	27	28	29	30	

MAY

S	M	T	W	T	F	S
						1
2	3	4	5	6	7	8
9	10	11	12	13	14	15
16	17	18	19	20	21	22
23	24	25	26	27	28	29
30	31					

APRIL

12 MONDAY

Cat's Eye
– Released 4-12-1985

13 TUESDAY

14 WEDNESDAY

THE LOST PROLOGUE

Director Lewis Teague has stated that there is a filmed prologue to *Cat's Eye* and that the studio cut it from the film. "... there is a prologue that I shot, and edited, that was cut out of the film, because the studio decided that was too far over the top, and it was over the top, I admit that, but I enjoyed it." Teague's description of the sequence is basically this: the cat in the film was living with a family only to wake up one morning to discover their daughter (played by Drew Barrymore) isn't breathing. The mother believed the old wives tale about cats stealing the breath of children and goes ballistic. While the father's on the phone with paramedics, and trying to revive his daughter, the mother has retrieved an automatic weapon from the father's gun collection and begins shooting up the house while chasing the cat she believes is the evil doer. The cat escapes through a broken glass window and is running for it's life. This is where the released version of the movie begins, where the cat is chased by a dog and almost run over by a car. What the audience would have discovered is that it was a tiny troll that was actually stealing the little girls breath.

APRIL

15 THURSDAY

Tax Day

16 FRIDAY

17 SATURDAY

18 SUNDAY

As the troll is now on the move looking for another victim, it discovers another little girl, also played by Drew Barrymore, and follows her home. The cat sees the troll enter this house and decides to also stay at the house to protect this next little girl. The prologue is finished, complete, and after all these years you would have thought some marketing genius at the studio would have had a special edition DVD or Blu-Ray released to take advantage of this, complete Teague and Stephen King's vision, and give the fans what we should have seen in the first place. Maybe someone out there will catch on and make it happen. At this point they'd have everything to gain. They'd better hurry because after thirty-five years, now *I'm* starting to run out of breath.

Katzenauge is the German *Cat's Eye* Blu-Ray

APRIL

19 MONDAY

20 TUESDAY

21 WEDNESDAY

Pet Sematary
– Released 4-21-1989

THE SPARROWS ARE FLYING...

George Romero's *The Dark Half* is an underrated film. Although I might not have picked Timothy Hutton for the role of the author, he turned in a good performance. They certainly transformed him well to be his "dark half" as George Stark. Amy Madigan, his wife in the film, did well, but unfortunately there's not much chemistry between them, still, that doesn't affect the film much as a whole. Stephen King's tale of Thad Beaumont's alter ego, a pseudonymous author, George Stark, whose novels are major commercial successes has come alive and wants to replace Thad in the real world, and he'll stop at nothing to attain it. Romero's take on this novel is a well thought out adaptation. When you can grasp the spirt of a novel in a two hour film, pulling in the twists and turns of King's mind, then you've done well. There are some King films I watch repeatedly more than others. Of course as most Stephen King fans certainly have surmised is that Thad Beaumont and his alter ego, George Stark, is an analogue to Stephen King's own experience with his own pseudonym, Richard Bachman. Stephen King published these gratuitous novels of violence on the side while publishing his other work at the same time. I hadn't watched *The Dark Half* in awhile until recently, and it still holds up as one of the better films in the King canon. I especially liked the ending. Wait... did you hear that? A fluttering...

APRIL

22 THURSDAY

23 FRIDAY

The Dark Half
– Released 4-23-1993

24 SATURDAY

25 SUNDAY

BEAUMONT RIDES AGAIN!

What does it say on young Thad Beaumont's t-shirt in the beginning of the film when he's typing a story? What is the title of the story that Thad is typing? What is Sheriff Pangborn's police vehicle license plate number and what does it signify?

Answers:

1. Castle Rock Junior High School.
2. Thad is writing / typing the story "Here There Be Tygers," an original short story by Stephen King that was first published in Ubris magazine, 1968.
3. The license plate reads "274" and the total of these numbers equal thirteen, which Stephen King has noted that he has a fear of, which is called Triskaidekaphobia. "When I'm writing, I'll never stop work if the page number is 13 or a multiple of 13; I'll just keep on typing till I get to a safe number." – Stephen King.

APRIL

26 MONDAY

27 TUESDAY

28 WEDNESDAY

CREEPSHOW 2 CREEP-A-ZOIDS!

Rick Wakeman, who was in the rock band, YES, co-wrote a lot of the music for this soundtrack with Les Reed. The soundtrack was eventually released for the first time in 2017, the 30th Anniversary of *Creepshow 2* in a double vinyl album set from Waxworks Records. The score, co-composed and performed by Les Reed and Rick Wakeman, features a mix of both classic, orchestral compositions and electronic, synth cues. After a lengthy search of the original masters, Waxwork Records was able to work directly with composers Les Reed and Rick Wakeman to acquire the original source material and re-master for vinyl. The album is available on 2 variants of color vinyl including "The Raft" (180 gram Coke Bottle Clear & Black Blob Vinyl) and "Old Chief Woodenhead" (180 gram Metallic Golden Brown & Deep Teal Swirl). There's also a "Hitchhiker" subscriber variant making this 3 versions released.

MAY

29 THURSDAY

30 FRIDAY

1 SATURDAY

Creepshow 2
– Released 5-1-1987

Kentucky Derby Day

2 SUNDAY

EYEBALLS SHAKEN... NOT STIRRED.

Actress Lois Chiles is featured in the segment, "The Hitchhiker." She also played a James Bond Girl! What James Bond film was she in? What is the name of her character? Who's behind all that makeup that plays The Creep in the introduction and at the end of the film?

Answers:

1. *Moonraker.*
2. Holly Goodhead.
3. Tom Savini was The Creep behind all that makeup.

APRIL

S	M	T	W	T	F	S
				1	2	3
4	5	6	7	8	9	10
11	12	13	14	15	16	17
18	19	20	21	22	23	24
25	26	27	28	29	30	

MAY

S	M	T	W	T	F	S
						1
2	3	4	5	6	7	8
9	10	11	12	13	14	15
16	17	18	19	20	21	22
23	24	25	26	27	28	29
30	31					

JUNE

S	M	T	W	T	F	S
		1	2	3	4	5
6	7	8	9	10	11	12
13	14	15	16	17	18	19
20	21	22	23	24	25	26
27	28	29	30			

MAY

3 MONDAY

4 TUESDAY

5 WEDNESDAY

Tales From the Darkside: The Movie
– Featuring Stephen King's
"The Cat From Hell"
– Released 5-4-1990

WHICH IS IT?

Tales From the Darkside… or… *Creepshow 3*? Director George Romero, and master horror makeup artist Tom Savini, have both discussed that *Tales From the Darkside* is considered by them to be the unofficial *Creepshow 3*. The director of *Tales From the Darkside* (1990), John Harrison, has been associated with George Romero productions for years, including the original *Creepshow* film and *Tales From the Darkside* TV series. He was the composer for *Creepshow* (1982) and directed eight TFTD TV episodes, including another Stephen King story, "Sorry Right Number" (under a pseudonym). With "The Cat From Hell," by Stephen King (screenplay by George Romero), in TFTD film Harrison is a part of the Stephen King film canon of work on several levels. "The Cat From Hell" was originally slated for *Creepshow 2*, but was cut due to budgetary reasons. The other episodes include "Lover's Vow" by Michael McDowell, and Lot 49" by Arthur Conan Doyle (screenplay also by Michael McDowell). I can only assume since this film was released 2 years after the end of the five year run of the TV series that it was the logical choice to release it under *Tales From the Darkside*.

Tales From the Darkside Collector's Edition Blu-Ray, 2020 from SHOUT! FACTORY

MAY

6 THURSDAY

7 FRIDAY

Sometimes They Come Back
– Released 5-7-1991

8 SATURDAY

9 SUNDAY

Mother's Day

SEX, & DRUGS, & . . . STEPHEN KING?

Betty, featured in the wraparound story in *Tales from the Darkside*, is played by a famous musician from the 70's and 80's. What is her name? What band did she front?

The "Cat From Hell" segment, based on Stephen King's original short story, has a soundtrack piece written and performed by a musician whose band gained prominence in the British music in the '70's and '80's. Who is the artist? What band was he a member of? The band has an original song that became an iconic line in music history. What is this song?

Answers:

1. Debbie Harry.
2. *Blondie*. This band had many hits including "One Way or Another," "Heart of Glass," "Rapture," and "Call Me," among many others.
3. Chaz Jankel is an original member of the band.
4. *Ian Dury and the Blockheads* and...
5. he also co-wrote their famous song, "Sex & Drugs & Rock & Roll," that became an iconic line since it's initial release in 1977, which was also their first single.

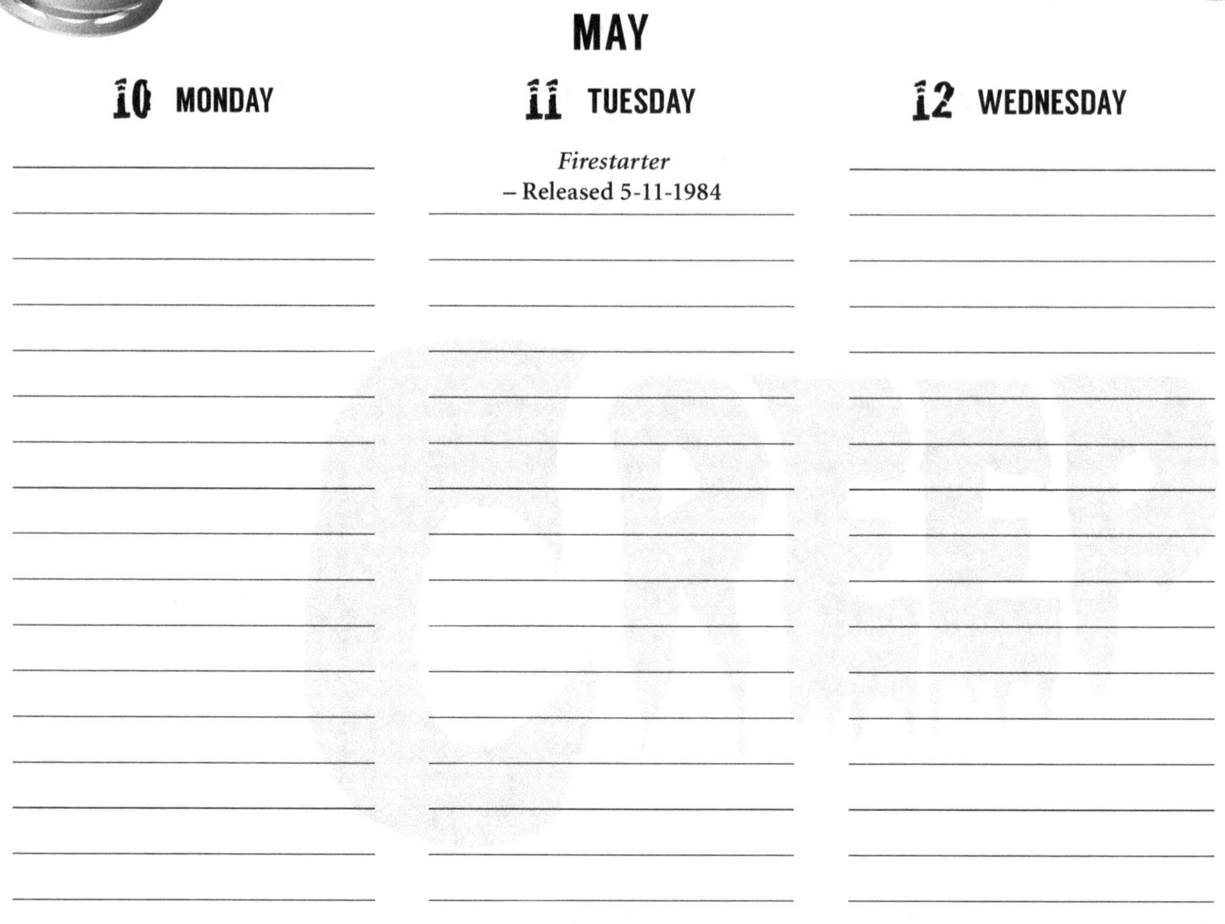

MAY

10 MONDAY

11 TUESDAY

Firestarter
– Released 5-11-1984

12 WEDNESDAY

"I'll teach you to throw away my comic books!" – Billy, *Creepshow*

The comic book featured in the original *Creepshow* film was (eeek!) never produced. Granted there was a beautiful full color trade paperback released for the film created by horror and fantasy artist, Bernie Wrightson, featuring Stephen King's stories from the film. However no real comic issue was ever published. Rick Catizone, who worked on *Creepshow*, and created the animation for the film, oversaw the comic made for the film. He has stated that artist Jack Kamen, an original EC Comics artist – of which *Creepshow* is a homage too, produced the cover of the comic and eight pages of black & white panel art. Then they took a real comic apart and inserted these pages within that comic to make it look like the size of an actual issue. They had to color the pages and then had them xeroxed onto newsprint for what you see used in the film. Then the Kamen cover was applied. Thus the pseudo *Creepshow* issue was born. Having Jack Kamen be a part of this project added authenticity to the project and showed just how far the filmmakers were willing to go to give the audience something special. It's obvious that this was close to the bleeding hearts and rotting minds of the creators and it shows. They grew up with EC Comics and they were able to express this "dark love" in the truly, now classic, horror anthology, *Creepshow*. Oh, and where did that comic from the film end up? It's currently owned by a private collector in the US, who collects *Creepshow* and horror items. He owns the large crate from the film as well.
I wonder if Fluffy ever comes out to play?

MAY

13 THURSDAY

Quicksilver Highway
– Released 5-13-1997

14 FRIDAY

15 SATURDAY

16 SUNDAY

Creepshow
– Released 5-16-1982

PIN CUSHION BILLY

What actor plays Billy in the prologue and epilogue of the film as it is listed in the credits? What relationship does he have to the author of *Creepshow*? What is his complete name?

Answers:

1. Joe King
2. He's is Stephen King's son, Joe.
3. Joe Hillstrom King.

APRIL

S	M	T	W	T	F	S
				1	2	3
4	5	6	7	8	9	10
11	12	13	14	15	16	17
18	19	20	21	22	23	24
25	26	27	28	29	30	

MAY

S	M	T	W	T	F	S
						1
2	3	4	5	6	7	8
9	10	11	12	13	14	15
16	17	18	19	20	21	22
23	24	25	26	27	28	29
30	31					

JUNE

S	M	T	W	T	F	S
		1	2	3	4	5
6	7	8	9	10	11	12
13	14	15	16	17	18	19
20	21	22	23	24	25	26
27	28	29	30			

MAY

17 MONDAY

18 TUESDAY

19 WEDNESDAY

THE OVERLOOK HOTEL has gained quite a reputation considering it's a fictional creation by Stephen King. This place has a haunted life of it's own and has shown quite a few guests, and caretakers, it's evil face throughout the decades. To create this hotel for the 1980 film was quite an under taking (no pun intended.. wink, wink) and that has a history all it's own. Let's see what you know from the following trivia questions about this, haunt.

1. **Stephen King and his family vacationed in Boulder, Colorado in the 70's. During their stay they spent one night at a different hotel in Colorado. The hotel was closing for the winter, so they were practically the only guests there and thus the seed was planted for what became his novel, *The Shining*. What is the name of this real hotel? Where is it located?**
2. **The exterior shot of The Overlook Hotel, for the 1980 Kubrick version of Stephen King's novel, was filmed at a real hotel. What is the name of this hotel and where is it located?**
3. **Some of the interior designs of the Overlook Hotel set were based on those of a hotel in Yosemite National Park. If you visit the lobby of this hotel you'll feel like you've walked onto *The Shining* set. What is the name of this hotel?**

MAY

20 THURSDAY

21 FRIDAY

22 SATURDAY

23 SUNDAY

The Shining
– Released 5-23-1980

Answers:

1. The Stanley Hotel. Estes Park, Colorado.
2. The Timberline Lodge, Mt. Hood, Oregon.
3. Ahwahnee Hotel, Yosemite Valley, California.

APRIL

S	M	T	W	T	F	S
				1	2	3
4	5	6	7	8	9	10
11	12	13	14	15	16	17
18	19	20	21	22	23	24
25	26	27	28	29	30	

MAY

S	M	T	W	T	F	S
						1
2	3	4	5	6	7	8
9	10	11	12	13	14	15
16	17	18	19	20	21	22
23	24	25	26	27	28	29
30	31					

JUNE

S	M	T	W	T	F	S
		1	2	3	4	5
6	7	8	9	10	11	12
13	14	15	16	17	18	19
20	21	22	23	24	25	26
27	28	29	30			

MAY

24 MONDAY

25 TUESDAY

26 WEDNESDAY

TALK ABOUT DULL.

Vivian Kubrick, Stanley Kubrick's daughter, discussed in her commentary on *Making 'The Shining'* (1980), that Margaret Adams, who's listed in the end credits as the director's secretary, was the person who typed up all the hundreds of various forms of "All Work and No Play Makes Jack a Dull Boy" pages that are used in the Stanley Kubrick movie of *The Shining*. Apparently this took her months to produce. The original prop box of yellow typing paper used in the film, with the phrase repeated over and over again of "All work and no play makes Jack a dull boy," is located in the Stanley Kubrick Archive in London.

MAY

27 THURSDAY

28 FRIDAY

29 SATURDAY

30 SUNDAY

About one-third of the stack was manually typed; the remainder was photocopied. There are also additional boxes in other languages as Kubrick had an idea to use these as well. Stanley Kubrick reportedly recorded the sound of a typist actually typing the words "All work and no play makes Jack a dull boy" due to the fact that each key on a typewriter sounds slightly different and he wanted to ensure authenticity in the scene.[1]

The Shining movie paperback release featuring the official movie cover art. 1980 Signet, New American Library edition.

APRIL

S	M	T	W	T	F	S
				1	2	3
4	5	6	7	8	9	10
11	12	13	14	15	16	17
18	19	20	21	22	23	24
25	26	27	28	29	30	

MAY

S	M	T	W	T	F	S
						1
2	3	4	5	6	7	8
9	10	11	12	13	14	15
16	17	18	19	20	21	22
23	24	25	26	27	28	29
30	31					

JUNE

S	M	T	W	T	F	S
		1	2	3	4	5
6	7	8	9	10	11	12
13	14	15	16	17	18	19
20	21	22	23	24	25	26
27	28	29	30			

JUNE

31 MONDAY
Memorial Day

1 TUESDAY

2 WEDNESDAY

Der Tod Fährt Mit translates to *Death Goes With You* the German translated title for the Blu-Ray edition of *Riding the Bullet.*

TIME FOR FUN!

"Fun is fun, and done is done."
- Stephen King, *Riding the Bullet.*

Where was this Stephen King original novella, *Riding the Bullet*, released? The nurse in the film, *Riding the Bullet*, has an iconic name in the Stephen King canon, that of Annie Wilkes. What other Stephen King story features this nurse? This nurse is acted by who in *Riding the Bullet*? The Apple Man in the film is a cameo by a musician who's had hits in the 60's and 70's with his band, and as a popular duo. Who is the Apple Man? Bonus question: Can you name his band and the duo he was a part of?

JUNE

3 THURSDAY

4 FRIDAY

5 SATURDAY

6 SUNDAY

Answers:

1. *Riding the Bullet* was released in 2000 as the worlds first mass market e-book on the internet and only available in that format for awhile.
2. The novel *Misery* features Annie Wilkes as the nurse that cares for the writer she discovers in an accident near her home.
3. Cynthia Garris, an actress who's appeared in several Stephen King film productions and is the wife of director, Mick Garris.
4. Howard Kaylan makes a cameo as the Apple Man and is one of the founding members of The Turtles, and the duo Flo and Eddie.

MAY

S	M	T	W	T	F	S
						1
2	3	4	5	6	7	8
9	10	11	12	13	14	15
16	17	18	19	20	21	22
23	24	25	26	27	28	29
30	31					

JUNE

S	M	T	W	T	F	S
		1	2	3	4	5
6	7	8	9	10	11	12
13	14	15	16	17	18	19
20	21	22	23	24	25	26
27	28	29	30			

JULY

S	M	T	W	T	F	S
				1	2	3
4	5	6	7	8	9	10
11	12	13	14	15	16	17
18	19	20	21	22	23	24
25	26	27	28	29	30	31

JUNE

7 MONDAY

8 TUESDAY

9 WEDNESDAY

CELL PHONE UPGRADE?

"I just finished a screenplay for *Cell* so maybe it will be done. I got so many complaints about the end of the book that I changed everything. I still like the zombies..."

– Stephen King, Dundalk, Maryland, during *Under the Dome* 2009 book tour. November 11th, 2009.

It had been originally announced in 2006 that director Eli Roth (*Hostel, Cabin Fever*) was set to direct the film of *Cell* for Dimension films. However by 2009 Roth and Dimension parted ways as they disagreed on how to approach the project. It was put on the back burner until in 2013 it was announced that Tod Williams, who previously directed *Paranormal Activity 2*, would now direct the project. Starring John Cusack and Samuel Jackson, both who'd enjoyed previous success in another Stephen King film, *1408*, had joined forces again in this new King production. It was filmed for the month of January 2014 in Atlanta. Since I live in the Atlanta area I looked into going to the set to see some of the filming and write about this new project.

JUNE

10 THURSDAY

Cell
– Released 6-10-2016

11 FRIDAY

12 SATURDAY

13 SUNDAY

After trying several avenues it seems this was a totally closed set. I even had others in the King community who got in touch with me as they were also trying to visit and report on the set. No response. It's not unheard of, but most films appreciate the attention you bring to their production, especially when the film is released. With nothing to report on or about the film the King fans waited patiently for a release date. As of February 2015 it was announced that it had been picked up by a distribution company. Then it was acquired again, this time by Saban Films. Two and a half years later it was finally released to video-on-demand with a limited theatrical run on July 8th, 2016. Obviously there were problems as the story is sort of lost in this production. Even with the talent of Cusack and Jackson it's apparent that not even they could save the story that was presented in this film. The critics, to say the least, were not kind and it has more or less just became a background film in the canon of King theatrical releases. Even with the changes to the screenplay vs. The book, by Stephen King, it seems the signal was lost. – Dave Hinchberger

JUNE

14 MONDAY

15 TUESDAY

16 WEDNESDAY

Der Feuerteufel translates to *The Fire Devil*, the German title for *The Firestarter* 2007 DVD release.

DID YOU KNOW?

Many eight-year-olds were interviewed to play the part of Charlie McGee for *Firestarter*. In fact Heather O'rourke of *Poltergeist* fame ("they're here!") was also considered and interviewed for the role. In the end it was between Heather and Drew (both were born the same year, 1975). However producer Dino De Laurentiis pushed for Drew Barrymore to take the lead as he saw her star rising in the film industry and thus Drew won the part of Charlie McGee. An interesting side note: Drew Barrymore was considered for the part of Carol in *Poltergeist*. She lost out to Heather O'rourke when Steven Spielberg discovered her at the MGM commissary having lunch with her family as her sister was filming a dance scene in *Pennies From Heaven*.

JUNE

17 THURSDAY

18 FRIDAY

19 SATURDAY

20 SUNDAY

Father's Day

AND THE AWARD GOES TO. . .

Did you know that not one, not two, but *three* Oscar winners appear in *Firestarter*? Who are they and what films did they win for?

Firestarter 2017 Scream Factory Collector's Blu Ray edition

Answers:

1. George C. Scott for Best Actor in *Patton*.
2. Louise Fletcher for Best Actress in *One Flew Over the Cuckoo's Nest*.
3. Art Carney won for Best Actor for *Harry and Tonto*. George C. Scott was paid one million dollars for three weeks work on *Firestarter*. The original budget was 10 million dollars but when they were able to get George C. Scott they threw in one million more dollars for his performance.

MAY

S	M	T	W	T	F	S
						1
2	3	4	5	6	7	8
9	10	11	12	13	14	15
16	17	18	19	20	21	22
23	24	25	26	27	28	29
30	31					

JUNE

S	M	T	W	T	F	S
		1	2	3	4	5
6	7	8	9	10	11	12
13	14	15	16	17	18	19
20	21	22	23	24	25	26
27	28	29	30			

JULY

S	M	T	W	T	F	S
				1	2	3
4	5	6	7	8	9	10
11	12	13	14	15	16	17
18	19	20	21	22	23	24
25	26	27	28	29	30	31

JUNE

21 MONDAY

22 TUESDAY

1408
– Released 6-22-2007

23 WEDNESDAY

Blockbuster Video, the immense rental chain, were given exclusive content for some of the movies they offered? Yes, and *1408* became a Blockbuster DVD exclusive with two alternate endings, an inside look with lead actor John Cusack on *1408*, as well as a look behind the scenes of the film. These extras were later added to special edition releases of *1408*, but Blockbuster did offer these exclusive extras initially to their customers. The disc and artwork were also produced exclusively for their stores. Blockbuster was a powerful video rental chain of 9,000 stores in the United States and around the world. They became a multi-billion dollar juggernaut in the video rental business and with that much of a customer base they were able to offer unique special editions to their customers.

JUNE

24 THURSDAY

25 FRIDAY

26 SATURDAY

27 SUNDAY

ENTER... IF YOU DARE!

Hotel Manager, Olin, and Mike Enslin enter the Dolphin Hotel elevator. What elevator music is playing? Who is the composer of this famous classical piece? As Mike Enslin enters room 1408 what does he exclaim? How does room 1408 announce itself to Mike Enslin?

Answers:

1. And the No. 13 strikes again! Eine kleine Nachtmusik[a] (Serenade No. 13 for strings in G major).
2. Performed by The Swedish Concert Orchestra in the film and composed by Wolfgang Amadeus Mozart.
3. 'This is, *it?*'
4. The radio on the bedside table suddenly begins playing "We've Only Just Begun," by The Carpenters, which startled him.

JUNE

28 MONDAY

29 TUESDAY

30 WEDNESDAY

DID YOU KNOW?

"Dolan's Cadillac" is an original novella by Stephen King. It was originally published in Castle Rock, Stephen King's official newsletter, in monthly installments as a serial story from February to June 1985. It was only available in this format until it was eventually published in his collection, *Nightmares and Dreamscapes*. The first four issues that included this story were xeroxed onto pre-made blank paper that included the title, *Castlerock*, which was in color. The last issue that completed the story was printed on the first issue that was produced in newsprint. The rest of the *Castlerock* newsletters were produced in newsprint for the rest of the publication.

JULY

1 THURSDAY

Dolan's Cadillac
– Released 7-1-2009

2 FRIDAY

3 SATURDAY

4 SUNDAY

Independence Day

A NOD TO POE

The line from *Dolan's Cadillac*, "For the love of God, Robinson!" is a direct reference to "For the love of God, Montresor!" from "The Cask of Amontillado" by Edgar Allan Poe. *Dolan's Cadillac* holds many ties to "The Cask of Amontillado," mainly in Robinson's burial of Dolan. This Poe story was an inspiration for *Dolan's Cadillac*. In Las Vegas Dolan stays at The Montressor Hotel, another nod to Poe's story.

Dolan's Cadillac Italian DVD release. Marketing line "uno terrificante storia di vendetta" translated says "a terrifying tale of revenge"

JUNE

S	M	T	W	T	F	S
		1	2	3	4	5
6	7	8	9	10	11	12
13	14	15	16	17	18	19
20	21	22	23	24	25	26
27	28	29	30			

JULY

S	M	T	W	T	F	S
				1	2	3
4	5	6	7	8	9	10
11	12	13	14	15	16	17
18	19	20	21	22	23	24
25	26	27	28	29	30	31

AUGUST

S	M	T	W	T	F	S
1	2	3	4	5	6	7
8	9	10	11	12	13	14
15	16	17	18	19	20	21
22	23	24	25	26	27	28
29	30	31				

JULY

5 MONDAY

6 TUESDAY

7 WEDNESDAY

Original Poster Design by Justin Froning
Houseboat Design thehousebear.com

REIMAGINED

I discovered a commissioned *Stand By Me* screenprint poster, a reimagining that I feel captures some of the heart of this beautiful story, tinged by the darkness that everyone in life encounters along this trail called life. A collaboration by Justin Froning and Josh Berwanger — artwork by Justin. "A scene that has always stood out to us is when Gordie is on night watch while the other boys sleep by the campfire. Gordie comes face to face with a fawn as they each appear to see something familiar deep within the other. His companions begin to awaken and he narrates, 'it was on the tip of my tongue to tell them about the deer, but I didn't. That was the one thing I kept to myself.' We all remember the train — the machine of life that moves forward on its course without emotion or remorse. It's the barrel of the gun. We can run, or we can stand it down. Either way, we see the fawn as youth, and when their trip is over, nothing will ever be the same again. 'I never had any friends later on like the ones I had when I was twelve. Jesus, does anyone?' – Stephen King, *Stand By Me* / 'The Body." Limited edition prints available at thehousebear.com and at darkcitygallery.com

JULY

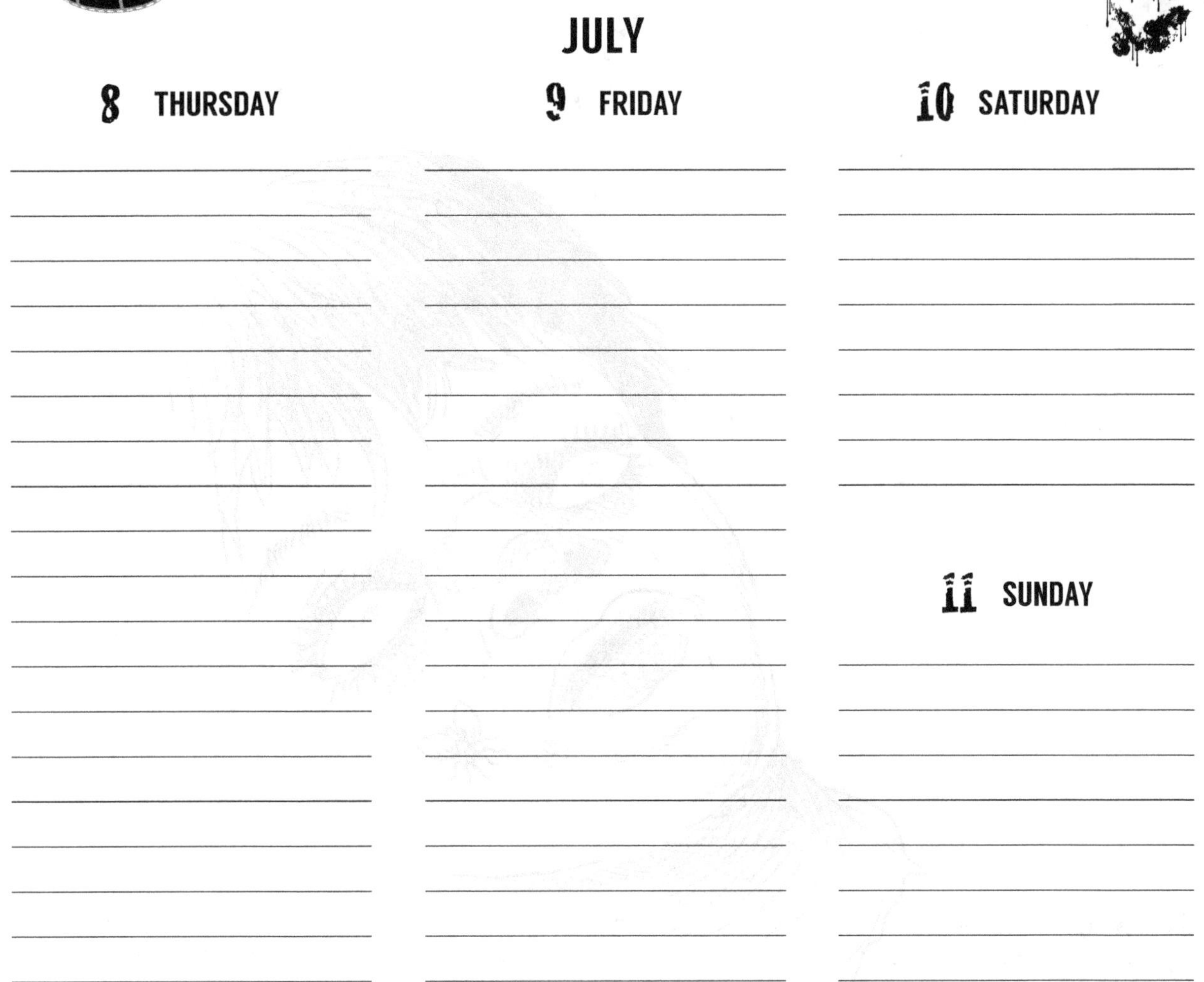

8 THURSDAY

9 FRIDAY

10 SATURDAY

11 SUNDAY

THE BODY WITHIN

What sub story appears within the novella, "The Body," and also in the film, *Stand By Me*? Where did this story make it's first published appearance?

Answers:

1. "The Revenge of Lard Ass Hogan."
2. The story first appeared The Maine Review, July, 1975. It was later incorporated into "The Body," published in the novella collection, *Different Seasons*, in 1982.

JUNE

S	M	T	W	T	F	S
		1	2	3	4	5
6	7	8	9	10	11	12
13	14	15	16	17	18	19
20	21	22	23	24	25	26
27	28	29	30			

JULY

S	M	T	W	T	F	S
				1	2	3
4	5	6	7	8	9	10
11	12	13	14	15	16	17
18	19	20	21	22	23	24
25	26	27	28	29	30	31

AUGUST

S	M	T	W	T	F	S
1	2	3	4	5	6	7
8	9	10	11	12	13	14
15	16	17	18	19	20	21
22	23	24	25	26	27	28
29	30	31				

JULY

12 MONDAY

13 TUESDAY

14 WEDNESDAY

Maximum Overdrive is a screenplay written by Stephen King, based on his own short story (see trivia next page) and his directorial debut. It is also the only film he's ever directed. The plot for the film shows the earth has crossed the path of a comet. Not long after machines of every type began to come to life on their own. People are attacked in various ways; people are electricuted, a waitress is injured by an electric knife that takes on a life of it's own. A soda vending machine kills a Little League coach by shooting a can at high speed into his skull (yes, this is in the film). Mowers run amuck, cars and trucks are killing throughout the town. At a truck stop (naturally, it's based on "Trucks" by Stephen King). A group of customers and employees, now stranded at the Dixie Boy Truck Stop, attempt to stay alive as they're trapped within by the vehicles circuling the truck stop, 24 hours a day. The vechicles devise a plan to continue to gas up as they hold the humans hostage. The film was a disaster, both critically and a bomb at the box office. Although after thirty-five years later it holds a certain B-movie charm, especially for delivering such inventive, gruesome deaths. The film was nominated for two Golden Raspberry Awards: including Worst Actor for Emilio Estevez and Worst Director for Stephen King in 1987, but both lost against Prince for his film, *Under the Cherry Moon*. Stephen King said he considered the film a learning experience [1]… after which he intended to never direct again [2]. Hey, you go with your strengths. His direction for novels is a field he knows how to bring to visual life for millions of happy readers. Who made who, indeed.

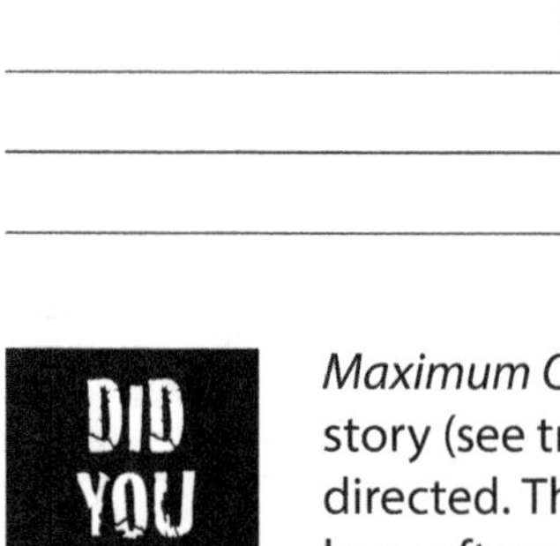

JULY

15 THURSDAY

Maximum Overdrive
– Released 7-15-1986

16 FRIDAY

17 SATURDAY

18 SUNDAY

TRIVIA:

1. What story is *Maximum Overdrive* based on by Stephen King?
2. The soundtrack for the film is by a famous hard rock act. Who… is this band?
3. What is the name of the title song they wrote / sang exlusively for the film?
4. What song is playing in the ice cream truck?

Answers:

1. Loosely based on the short story, "Trucks," by Stephen King.
2. AC/DC
3. "Who Made Who"
4. "King of the Road" by Roger Miller. An obvious nod to Stephen King himself.

JUNE

S	M	T	W	T	F	S
		1	2	3	4	5
6	7	8	9	10	11	12
13	14	15	16	17	18	19
20	21	22	23	24	25	26
27	28	29	30			

JULY

S	M	T	W	T	F	S
				1	2	3
4	5	6	7	8	9	10
11	12	13	14	15	16	17
18	19	20	21	22	23	24
25	26	27	28	29	30	31

AUGUST

S	M	T	W	T	F	S
1	2	3	4	5	6	7
8	9	10	11	12	13	14
15	16	17	18	19	20	21
22	23	24	25	26	27	28
29	30	31				

JULY

19 MONDAY

20 TUESDAY

21 WEDNESDAY

Pet Cemetery Spanish DVD. *El Cementerio Viviente* translates to *The Living Cemetery*

SOMETIMES... DEAD IS BETTER

Who plays the minister at the funeral held at a cemetery? What band wrote and sang the title song for the film? One more song by the band made it on the soundtrack. Which song? Mrs. Creed is hitchhiking after her car breaks down. She's given a ride by a trucker. What is the number on his cab?

Answers:

1. Stephen King performs the funeral, bible in hand, at a real cemetery local to Bangor, Maine, where the author lives.
2. The Ramones wrote and performed „Pet Sematary." Stephen King has been a long time fan of the band and asked them if they'd write a song for the film. It was one of the biggest hits of their career, even though it was nominated for the Razzie Award in 1989 (now defunct).
3. "Sheena is a Punk Rocker."
4. 666 is outside on the panel below the passenger side.

JULY

22 THURSDAY

23 FRIDAY

24 SATURDAY

25 SUNDAY

DID YOU KNOW?

George Romero was originally slated to direct *Pet Sematary*, and paid Stephen King $10,000 for the option in 1984.[1] Romero was involved with his film, *Monkey Shines*, and had to leave the production early on (I would have liked to have seen that version). [2] Not only is it based on Stephen King's novel, he wrote the screenplay and he had final say on the director. He also stipulated that the story would be filmed in Maine, which it was, in Bangor and surrounding areas. After meeting Mary Lambert, who agreed to stay faithful to the book, he was so impressed that he gave her the directing job.[3] Mary Lambert was primarily a video music director before taking the helm as the *Pet Sematary* director. She directed huge video hits with artists Madonna, Sting, Janet Jackson, The Go-Go's, The Eurythmics, Rod Stewart, and Queensrÿche to name just a few. She's also credited with bringing the Ramones on board to produce a song for the film, along with Stephen King. She knew them from being in the music biz. Elle Creed, the daughter, was played by twins Blaze and Beau Berdahl.

KING GOES INTO OVERDRIVE

First-time Director King Puts the Pedal to the Metal.

by Tyson Blue

Dusk. As I drive the coastal plains of North Carolina, I sense something ominous in the air. A huge truck, its lights glaring in my rear view mirror, roars behind me. Phil Collins on the radio feels it in the night, too:

"If you told me you were drowning, I would not lend a hand."

I pull into the Dixie Boy Truck Stop which, like so many others in this part of the Southeast, offers cheap fast food for people on the run. Only it doesn't look quite right.

The gravel lot is littered with semis, their trailers torn open, contents spilling out. A car, its windshield shattered, lies atop flat tires in a welter of garbage. And around the restaurant rolls a steady parade of hulking vehicles, even an ornate Peterbilt truck from Happy Toyz, Marvel Comics' Green Goblin emblazoned on its hood.

The Dixie Boy doesn't serve any grease-burgers, though. It's actually the set of *Overdrive*, the latest in the long series of De Laurentiis films based on the novels and short stories of Stephen King.

Overdrive is different, though. For the first time, King himself is directing.

"I figure that as far as films go, I'm back where I was when *The Dead Zone* came out in hardcover," King says, explaining why he has decided to direct. "Ever since *The Shining*, the films have gone down at the box office. It's not that they were all bad pictures; they just didn't do that well. So I thought that maybe if I directed the picture, it might pick things up."

In recent years King has often quoted John Updike's dictum that the best scenario for a writer requires that Hollywood buy his novel and never make the picture. Yet King is taking on the film business himself now.

Isn't he putting himself in the worst possible position?

"In terms of reputation, I am," King agrees. "But in terms of trying to find out whether or not I can actually do it, I'm in the only position I can be in. I mean, sooner or later this was bound to come up because there have been so many movies made from the stuff and maybe three or four have been well reviewed."

The Green Goblin mounted Happy Toyz Truck, the main villain of *Maximum Overdrive*. Photo DEG 1986, (De Laurentiis Entertainment Group)

The patrons of the Dixie Boy Truck Stop. Featuring L to R: Emilio Estevez, Leon Rippy, Pat Hingle, Robert Gooden, Ellen McElduff, Laura Harrington, Christopher Murney. (DEG 1986)

The Dixie Boy Truck Stop. (DEG 1986)

King, an admirer of Elmore Leonard, speaks with dismay about the film adaptation of Leonard's *Stick*.

"I want to tell the story that's between the lines," King explains. "I keep going back to seeing the movie Stick, with Burt Reynolds. I have a lot of Elmore Leonard books on my shelf. He's like me in a way—he tells stories that are interesting. I shouldn't say that about myself, but I think I tell stories that people want to read, they want to turn the next page. Anyway, whatever there is that's Elmore Leonard is between the lines–that's where the tension is.

"I waited three months to see this movie," he goes on, "and this is the first time I've done that since *Close Encounters of the Third Kind*. I was there for the first show, and I really wanted to see it because he did the screenplay, and I read the book and really liked it—and he wasn't there, you know?

"There's some of me in a lot of the pictures," he admits. "There's some in *Children of the Corn*, and there's a lot in *Cujo*. But there's no Stephen King in *Firestarter*. I'm not in that movie at all, whatever it was in the book that people liked. So I thought maybe if they let me alone, and let me make—the picture, it might work out."

Evidently, Alan Ladd of MGM and the De Laurentiis people have left him completely free to make his movie.

"They've let me make my picture," he says simply.

Based on the short story "Trucks," which appeared in the *Night Shift* anthology, Overdrive is a '"mechanical version of *The Birds*. In the story, a group of people are trapped in a truck stop by sentient eighteen-wheelers which run down anyone who tries to escape, forcing the survivors to fill their tanks.

For the film, King elaborated on the concept. "The premise became 'What if everything mechanical went bullshit?'" King says. "In this version, not just trucks, but lawnmowers, electric knives, everything comes alive. Next we needed a reason why. It wasn't very important, but we had the earth pass through a comet."

The film, which stars Emilio Estevez and Pat Hingle, is being shot on location outside of Wilmington, North Carolina, the home base of De Laurentiis's North Carolina Film Corporation. A full-scale truck stop, covering several acres, has been built from the ground up in painstaking detail, but the masterpiece is the restaurant itself.

So realistic is the set, which is built on the main artery between Wilmington and the Interstate highways inland, that drivers often pull in for fuel and food, overlooking the wrecked trucks, lights, reflectors, and movie-

Cameo appearance of Stephen King, author and director of *Maximum Overdrive*, at the ATM in Wilmington, North Carolina. Photo DEG, 1986.

Wanda June (Ellen McElduff) is attacked by a living electric knife. (DEG 1986)

Stephen King slates a scene with what appears to be the world's largest clapperboard. (DEG 1986)

Bill Robinson (Emilio Estevez) is forced to gas up the Happy Toyz Truck. (DEG 1986)

Director, Stephen King, shows actress Ellen McElduff how to sling hash. (DEG 1986)

making paraphernalia.

Estevez, star of the cult film *Repo Man*, plays Bill Robinson, a parolee working at the Dixie Boy, which is owned by Hindershot (Hingle). Hingle, who appeared as the irascible police chief in Clint Eastwood's *Sudden Impact*, gives neophyte director King high marks on his performance.

"He's doing a fabulous job," Hingle enthused. "This is a complicated picture, as you can see. "But he's doing very well. He's not a first time director who comes in and thinks he's John Ford."

Hingle is no stranger to fantasy roles. He has already filmed *Santa '85*, an episode of Steven Spielberg's *Amazing Stories*.

King freely admits that the intricacies of directing are new to him.

"What surprised me most about this was how little I knew," he says. "I knew how a film shouldn't look. I thought I'd just ease into this like cold water, a little at a time. This is earn while you learn," he chuckles.

Flexible with his performers, he is open to improvisation by the actors. "I feel that in film, I should be open to it, and when it comes I shouldn't feel the need to reject it."

One device King has rejected is the storyboard. Although some were made early on in the picture, they have not been used. They are too similar to plot outlines, which King has never used. Sometimes, however, he toys with a large tabletop model of the set to visualize sequences.

Asked about his influences, King names only one: Hitchcock.

Hitchcock, King says, was concerned with creating suspense rather than shock in his films. He cites the famous Hitchcock example of the men with the bomb under the table. If we know there's a bomb there and the men don't, and the scene lasts for ten minutes, we have ten minutes of tension.

"We do something like that early on in the film," King says. "We have a guy outside pumping gas, and all of a sudden the pumps stop. He cuts off the automatic device and looks at it, then digs around with his finger, trying to get dirt out of the line. Then he looks into the nozzle. We all know what's going to happen—he's going to get sprayed with gasoline—but we don't know when. I had him put the nozzle back down, then did it. It's all a matter of timing, and that creates suspense."

Despite his so-far happy directing experience, King doesn't plan to give up his word processor on a permanent basis.

"Oh God, no," he groans. "I can imagine doing it again sometime, but not very soon. I've got a family to take care of!"

For now, King is concentrating on impressing his vision of a mechanical world gone mad on America's film audience. He is confident that he can do so.

"Dino came by the set one day, and he was convinced we were making some kind of existential comedy film here," he recalls. "But I think that when everything is all done, we will have laughed our way to making a very scary film."

If it succeeds, *Overdrive* will make your skin crawl every time a truck creeps up behind you on the road.

JULY

26 MONDAY

27 TUESDAY

28 WEDNESDAY

DO YOU KA-TET?

In The Dark Tower film Jake and The Gunslinger stop over at an ancient site that was previously an amusement park. What is the name of the amusement park? At one point, Roland, The Gunslinger, comes across a door with a poster on it. Who is it? A mother, son, and dog are walking in New York City. What reference is this for? What car is Jake Chambers playing with in his room? Two girls in blue are shown, paying homage to what Stephen King film? A smiley face is drawn on Jake's room wall, with the words "Hello there," referencing what film / book? There's a book sitting up against equipment where The Dark Man is typing. What is this book and what novel is it from? Above one of the portals that Jake is about to go through shows what numbers?

JULY

29 THURSDAY

30 FRIDAY

31 SATURDAY

1 SUNDAY

Answers:

1. Pennywise
2. Rita Hayworth, who is on the poster in *The Shawshank Redemption* that Andy Defresne keeps on the wall in his prison cell.
3. The street scene from *The Dark Tower* (passing the Forbidden Planet comics shop in Manhattan), the two actors walking their dog actually bear a passing resemblance to Dee Wallace and Danny Pintauro from the 1983 movie, *Cujo*.
4. *Christine*, as a toy car.
5. The twins shown from the Breaker village, wearing blue t-shirts, with jean skirts represent the Grady Twins from *The Shining*.
6. *Mr. Mercedes*.
7. Misery's Child, from the novel *Misery*.
8. 14-08 obviously referencing the story / film *1408*. If you saw more references, we'd love to hear from you! E-mail ServiceOverlook@gmail.com

THE GUNSLINGER

AUGUST

2 MONDAY

3 TUESDAY

4 WEDNESDAY

The Dark Tower
– Released 8-4-2017

...NO, WE CAN'T DANCE TOGETHER

Very early in the movie, *The Dark Tower*, on the first building you see in Mid-World, what number is represented on it? What have the kids written on the playground in chalk? What number does Jake type into the portal computer keyboard? Where does this first portal take Jake to? There is a photo of the Overlook Hotel in the film of *The Dark Tower*. Where in the film is it located?

AUGUST

5 THURSDAY

6 FRIDAY

7 SATURDAY

8 SUNDAY

Answers:

1. 19 – 19.
2. 19 – 19, over and over again.
3. 19 – 19.
4. Mid world.
5. It's framed and sits on a shelf in Jake's therapist's office.

JULY

S	M	T	W	T	F	S
				1	2	3
4	5	6	7	8	9	10
11	12	13	14	15	16	17
18	19	20	21	22	23	24
25	26	27	28	29	30	31

AUGUST

S	M	T	W	T	F	S
1	2	3	4	5	6	7
8	9	10	11	12	13	14
15	16	17	18	19	20	21
22	23	24	25	26	27	28
29	30	31				

SEPTEMBER

S	M	T	W	T	F	S
			1	2	3	4
5	6	7	8	9	10	11
12	13	14	15	16	17	18
19	20	21	22	23	24	25
26	27	28	29	30		

AUGUST

9 MONDAY

10 TUESDAY

11 WEDNESDAY

Doctor Sleep
– Released 8-11-2019

IS IT HOT IN HERE OR IS IT ME?

I was a bit of a nerdy young teenager in the Summer of 1983. Life during that Summer was pretty carefree. It was all Dungeons & Dragons, video games and of course, movies. I remember the movie *Cujo* opened on a Friday. On Saturday, the second day of opening weekend, I convinced my folks that we should go see this new scary Stephen King flick. Gladly, they obliged for a late afternoon matinee showing. It was a broiling, muggy hot day as we arrived at the old Campus Twin Cinema in Columbia, Missouri, where I grew up. Now the Campus Twin was a really small place. In the tiny main street building were two side by side 'twin' theaters. Each theater sat around 50 people or so. The tiny lobby was crammed with lines… concession lines, screening lines… I bet the bathroom had lines! We bought our tickets, waiting patiently in the lobby when the theater manager asked for everyone's attention. He announced that the AC had just gone out and they didn't know how long it would take to get it repaired. He said "It's probably going to get real hot in here." He asked that if people wanted a refund to come to the box office or, if you wanted to stay and watch the screening you could and they would provide a free pass for a future movie ticket as a gesture of goodwill for the inconvenience. My folks and I mulled it over and

AUGUST

12 THURSDAY

Cujo
– Released 8-12-1983

13 FRIDAY

14 SATURDAY

15 SUNDAY

decided to stay and watch the show - hoping it wouldn't get *too* hot… It was mid August though - and that particular day was one of the 'Dog Days' of Summer. Those kind of days where the temperature is in the 90's, humidity is high and no breeze. Just a sticky, oven-like mess.

A few moments later, we were in the theater, grabbing some seats. Things felt okay — tolerable at least for the moment. As the movie proceeded, you could feel the still air in the theater becoming hotter and increasingly uncomfortable.

As the *Cujo* storyline progresses, an important and agonizing scene unfolds with characters Donna (Dee Wallace) and her son, Tad (Danny Pintauro) trapped in a small, cramped car, a Pinto (remember those?) at an isolated farm in the Summer heat. We ourselves were sweating along with them as the formerly sweet and huge St. Bernard, Cujo, now fully rabid, rampages against them, forcing them to stay in the now sweltering vehicle. Donna cracks the car windows to try to get some relief from the deteriorating conditions. Overhead, the hot sun makes the situation unbearable. It was like we were in an interactive movie as we could 'feel' the rising temperatures pictured on screen.

After further harrowing and sweltering, the movie concluded and we moved to the exit doors. I still remember walking outside and the feeling of relief - similar to the 'ahhh' moment when you walk out of a sauna. Dog days indeed.

– Bryan McAllister

1983 *Cujo* movie cover paperback edition, featuring the movie poster artwork. 1983 Signet, New American Library.

AUGUST

16 MONDAY

17 TUESDAY

18 WEDNESDAY

DANNY CAM

Danny Lloyd, who played Danny Torrance in Stanley Kubrick's *The Shining*, makes a cameo appearance as a spectator at Bradley Trevor's baseball game. Danny Lloyd has been retired from acting for almost forty years. Director Mike Flanagan found him on Twitter and Lloyd leapt at the chance to appear in the film. Lloyd, 47 when he came in for his cameo, currently has a very successful career as a schoolteacher. He was able to come back to act for a day to be in *Doctor Sleep*. Producer Trevor Macy was asked why Jack Nicholson wasn't in for a cameo. Macy said, "With Jack, I knew that they approached him for *Ready Player One*, and that he seems to be very serious about being retired. I had known that he was supportive [of the sequel] but retired."[1] Mike Flanagan admitted it wouldn't have been easy to have Nicholson in the sequel. "I didn't know how that would really work," Flanagan said. "Even if he were to come back, if he were appearing as a different character, I thought that would set people's hair on fire. … He was absolutely a presence on set, though, whether he knew it or not."

AUGUST

19 THURSDAY

20 FRIDAY

21 SATURDAY

22 SUNDAY

Stand by Me
– Released 8-22-1986

Doctor Sleep Director, Mike Flanagan, and crew placed a lot of references, or rather 'Easter Eggs,' in the film. The unblinking eyes. In the Jack Torrance sequence —unblinking eyes. "You'll notice when you watch that scene again, he never blinks," Flanagan says of the spectral character. Did you realize that in Kubrick's *The Shining* none of the ghosts blink? "You might watch that movie a hundred times and wonder why you're so affected by Lloyd the bartender, by Delbert Grady… that they never blinked. That's a level of genius. What you expect to be natural and human about those interactions isn't, and that's magical Kubrick. You can't even put your finger on why it's so uncanny and why it disturbs you so much." said Mike Flanagan. Musical egg: All the music played on the radio is a direct reference to music from *The Shining*. Flanagan said. Big Wheel egg: When young Danny is riding his big wheel through the Overlook's halls in Kubrick's *Shining* the wheels were extra loud on the hardwood floors and then became hushed when the he rolled over the carpet. When the villains, The True Knot, are driving through the woods in *Doctor Sleep* they drive off of a gravel road onto a paved road, repeating the Big Wheel effect. Room egg: Dan Torrance, working in an old age home, uses his psychic abilities comforting the folks about to pass over. The first patient he visits is in Room 217, an obvious nod to the novels original room number.

AUGUST

23 MONDAY

24 TUESDAY

25 WEDNESDAY

FROM SAINT TO SINNER.

"Max (Von Sydow) was a pure joy to work with"
– Fraser Heston, Director, *Needful Things*.

The *Needful Things* director, Fraser Heston, is the son of actor Charlton Heston (*Ben Hur, The Omega Man, Planet of the Apes*). In the film *The Greatest Story Ever Told* Von Sydow played Jesus, and Charlton Heston was John the Baptist. In this film Heston baptised Von Sydow in the river. In *Needful Things* Von Sydow, playing Leland Gaunt, is inferred to be Satan, although he's never called that by name. The irony here is Von Sydow previously played Jesus, and was baptised by the director's father, Charlton Heston. Decades later Von Sydow then plays Satan for Charlton Heston's son, Fraser. At moments like this, lightning strikes could be imminent…!

AUGUST

26 THURSDAY

27 FRIDAY

Needful Things
– Released 8-27-1993

28 SATURDAY

29 SUNDAY

PLAY HARDBALL

The baseball card that young Brain Rusk in the *Needful Things* film prized, and had to earn from LeLand Gaunt, featured which player? Which baseball player was originally used in the novel by Stephen King?

Answers:

1. Mickey Mantle.
2. Sandy Koufax. "We decided to use a Mickey Mantle card as he was the most well known baseball card we could come up with (to relate to a wider audience)." - Fraser Heston, Director of *Needful Things*. Out of curiosity I looked up how much a 1956 Sandy Koufax baseball card is worth in 2020. I found over 300 cards at one auction site and based on condition it began at $31.00 starting bid to $7,500 and you could purchase that last one outright at $49,000. Being a collector myself, I now understand young Brian's interest and how he got sucked in by Gaunt.

AUGUST

30 MONDAY

31 TUESDAY

1 WEDNESDAY

THE RAT PACK

What is the name of the story that the film *Graveyard Shift* is based on? When and where was it first published? What book is the character, Ippeston, reading in the booth behind John and Jane when they're in the cafe together?

Answers:

1. "Graveyard Shift"
2. *Cavalier* magazine, October 1970.
3. *Ben* by Gilbert S. Ralston. *Ben* features a colony of rats that's headed by Ben who's befriended by a young boy named, Danny. Ben's rat colony eventually becomes violent that results in several human deaths and is an obvious nod in *Graveyard Shift* which has, to say the least, it's own rat issues.

SEPTEMBER

2 THURSDAY

3 FRIDAY

4 SATURDAY

5 SUNDAY

THE MAINE THING

Graveyard Shift was filmed in Maine, Stephen King's home state and where he's had some success having his stories filmed there. They shot the movie in Harmony, Maine, and in the historic Bartlett mill, the oldest wool mill in the United States, in business since 1821. This mill was renamed "Bachman Mill" an homage to King's pseudonym, Richard Bachman. The interior shots of the antique mill machinery, and the riverside cemetery, were in Harmony. Other scenes filmed, a restaurant interior, and a giant wool picking machine, were at locations in Bangor, Maine, at an abandoned waterworks and armory. A few other mill scenes were staged near the Eastland woolen mill in Corinna, Maine. This mill subsequently became a Superfund site. A Superfund site is designated by the EPA and is designed to investigate and clean up sites contaminated with hazardous substances. About 40,000 Superfund sites exist in the US. They say for films it's all about location. Talk about the real kill feel, at that mill, huh? Stephen King disliked the film and named it one of his least favorite adaptations calling it "a quick exploitation picture".[1]

AUGUST

S	M	T	W	T	F	S
1	2	3	4	5	6	7
8	9	10	11	12	13	14
15	16	17	18	19	20	21
22	23	24	25	26	27	28
29	30	31				

SEPTEMBER

S	M	T	W	T	F	S
			1	2	3	4
5	6	7	8	9	10	11
12	13	14	15	16	17	18
19	20	21	22	23	24	25
26	27	28	29	30		

OCTOBER

S	M	T	W	T	F	S
					1	2
3	4	5	6	7	8	9
10	11	12	13	14	15	16
17	18	19	20	21	22	23
24	25	26	27	28	29	30
31						

SEPTEMBER

6 MONDAY

IT Chapter 2
– Released 9-6-2019

7 TUESDAY

8 WEDNESDAY

IT Chapter 1
– Released 9-8-2017

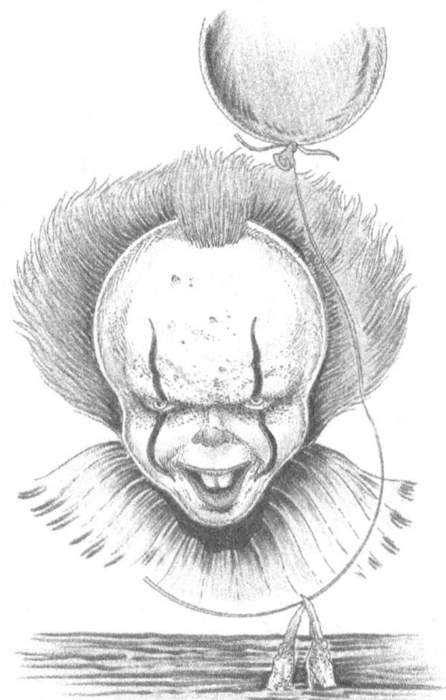

Andy Muschietti's *IT* – Friends and Fear

Stephen King's story of The Loser's Club against a supernatural clown has had its hooks in me since the 1990 TV miniseries. What Andy Muschietti did for his two-film adaptation of King's story is bring it into a modern world, and bring in some of King's loopier supernatural concepts while keeping the Losers front-and-center. It's an approach that doesn't always work, especially in the second film, but it makes for a more sinister film, where the success of the Losers is not assured by narrative conventions. If the second film doesn't work as well as the first film in Muschietti's series, it's because, like in the earlier miniseries, the material with the group as children is so much more potent than when they have to come together as adults. Putting children, who are all outcasts, together to face Pennywise feeds into some very basic genre tropes that go all the way back to a film like *Night of the Hunter* or the "Hansel & Gretel" fairy tale. When the adults come back, they just have to remember that connection they had as children, and use the

SEPTEMBER

9 THURSDAY

10 FRIDAY

11 SATURDAY

12 SUNDAY

intelligence they've gained growing older, to defeat a villain more suited to terrify children than adults. One of the things *Chapter Two* does so well, though, is giving us a clearer view of the PTSD each character has struggled with since childhood, and repressed those feelings. It grounds the film in an emotional connection that is so important to keep the story from being ridiculous. The moments that are supposed to work in terms of terror and suspense keep us on the edge of our seats, all the while keeping us invested in the characters. Pennywise is a villain that can represent anything you want, and is able to shift into any form that will fear its victim most. The clown is an iconic representation of evil in this story, and there is something to be said about the ways both Tim Curry and Bill Skarsgard bring the character to life. In Muschietti's vision, Skarsgard's sinister facial expressions and eyes are as haunting as anything we've seen in a King adaptation since Nicholson's Jack Torrence in *The Shining*. We understand acutely why he would haunt The Loser's Club from childhood to adulthood. In the end, though, it's the bond between the Losers that will get them through, and it's why both chapters of Muschietti's adaptation of this iconic Stephen King story will endure over the years. – Brian Skuttle

SEPTEMBER

13 MONDAY

Horrorstory (1408, India)
– Released 9-13-2013

14 TUESDAY

15 WEDNESDAY

DID YOU KNOW?

There is a Bollywood film, an Indian version based on *1408*, titled *Horror Story*. A group of friends learn about an abandoned hotel that is reportedly haunted and decide to seek it out. Originally a mental asylum for the criminally insane, it was essentially destroyed in an unexplained fire. After years of neglect, the ruins were refurbished into a five star hotel by a new owner. The hotel had many strange disturbances and eventually the owner committed suicide under mysterious circumstances. The group enter the building and think they hear "welcome," as they arrive. They come across a TV set that is transmitting but isn't plugged in. They proceed to a notorious room of hauntings, 3046, where the first of several deaths occur in the hotel. The group realizes no matter where they go they end up back at room 3046. This film was written by Vikram Bhatt, Mohan Azad, and Sukhmani Sadana. It was released on September 13, 2013. And… 3046 adds up to… you got it… 13.

SEPTEMBER

16 THURSDAY

Yom Kippur

17 FRIDAY

18 SATURDAY

19 SUNDAY

KEEPING UP APPEARANCES

What book is actress Candy Clark reading in bed? What dog chases the cat in the beginning of *Cat's Eye*? The cat is almost hit by a car during the chase scene with the dog. What is the car? Bonus question: What does the bumper sticker read on the car?

Answers:

1. *Pet Sematary*
2. *Cujo*, a St. Bernard, and a Stephen King novel.
3. Plymouth, Fury. Bonus: Watch out for me I am Pure Evil I am CHRISTINE.

SEPTEMBER

20 MONDAY

21 TUESDAY

22 WEDNESDAY

DID YOU BRING THE HANDCUFFS?

Where was *Gerald's Game* filmed? *Gerald's Game* was produced exclusively for Netflix. However it did have a theatrical release. When and where was *Gerald's Game* shown? Mike Flanagan made another Stephen King film after *Gerald's Game*. Which film?

Answers:

1. 90% of *Gerald's Game* was filmed in Mobile, Alabama.
2. *Gerald's Game* made it's worldwide theatrical debut at the British Film Institute theater, September 19, 2017. It was then released ten days later on Netflix September 29, 2017.
3. *Doctor Sleep*.

SEPTEMBER

23 THURSDAY

The Shawshank Redemption
– Released 9-23-1994

24 FRIDAY

25 SATURDAY

26 SUNDAY

Children of the Corn 2009
– Released 9-26-2009

"I've wanted to make this story since I was 19. I'm a Stephen King fanatic. When I was in college I read the book and thought it was amazing but unfilmable. Half my life I've been trying to make this movie." – Mike Flanagan, Director, *Gerald's Game*.

Reading this line just took me back to my first reading of *Gerald's Game*. I was not impressed. Halfway through the book I was struggling to continue. My part-timer at the bookstore, Chuck, who shipped all our books, asked me what I thought of it. I couldn't give him an answer really as I'd hadn't finished the book. I wasn't getting it. He said, "hey, when you're done, my sister really wants to read it, can I borrow it then?" He went home with it that night. I thought if she really wants to read it, fine, I can go back to it later but right now I'll take a break. Sometimes you have to put a book down and let it sink in, if it ever does. I'm a firm believer of finishing a novel or film. How can you truly review something that you haven't completed? You can say you hadn't finished it, not your "cup of tea," as they say, but a complete review? No. Mike Flanagan, and his lead actress (well, she's the actress, period, right?), Carla Gugino, made this into one great story. She really pulls it off. Flanagan and Jeff Howard's tight writing, and bringing this story to the screen was, to put it lightly, genius. It works better than the novel, at least their version is something I could really, you know, sink my teeth into.. From one King fan to all of us, "constant readers," a gift for the King fans to be sure.

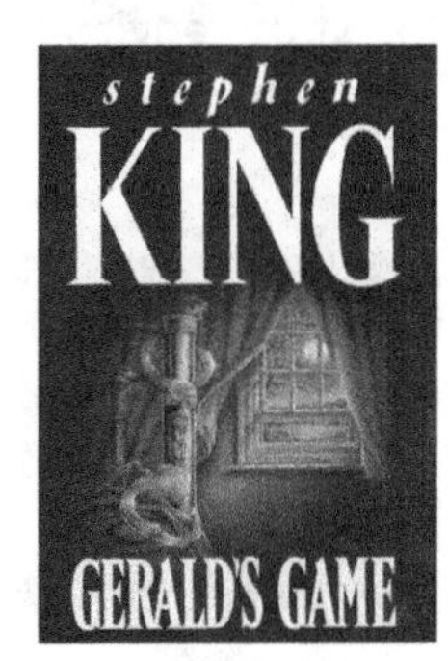

Gerald's Game First Printing, Hodder & Stoughton, London, 1993.

SEPTEMBER

27 MONDAY

28 TUESDAY

Hearts in Atlantis
– Released 9-28-2001

HAVE YOU SEEN
BRAUTIGAN?
HE'S AN OLD MONGREL
BUT WE LOVE HIM.
Brautigan Has Grey Fur
And Blue Eyes
LARGE REWARD
($$$$$$)
If You Have Seen Him Call
Housitonic 5-837

29 WEDNESDAY

Gerald's Game
– Released 9-29-2017

"We're all just passing through, kiddo." – Ted Brautigan

Some director's of Stephen King films have been able to take an essence of a story and transform it into something special. A few films that have accomplished this is Rob Reiner's *Stand by Me*, Frank Darabont's *The Shawshank Redemption*, and Scott Hick's *Hearts in Atlantis*. I feel they all took King's material and created something unique for the audience, and for the author. Stephen King infuses his work with styles, music, and surroundings that he grew up with. I swear sometimes you can injest the environment he pulls you into with his storytelling. That's what makes Stephen King so good at weaving tales. Director Scott Hicks had a unique job though with *Hearts in Atlantis*. This collection of novellas, what Stephen King has referred too as his "Vietnam book," isn't something easily made into just, one film. Hicks was able to pull out a unique perspective to give us on the big screen. He said "It was the halcyon days of 1960 but a lot was going on under the surface" and you can feel that in his film. *Hearts in Atlantis* captures an innocent time, that a lot of us can remember when we were young. Imagine a weekend day, no worries except what TV show you're going to watch, playing sports with friends, listening to records in your room, all in the course of a sunny day where your future isn't even a thought. You're living for the joy of today. The romanticism is tangent here in Hicks vision. The longing

HAVE YOU SEEN
BRAUTIGAN?
HE'S AN OLD MONGREL
BUT WE LOVE HIM.
Brautigan Has Grey Fur
And Blue Eyes
LARGE REWARD
($$$$$$)
If You Have Seen Him Call
Housitonic 5-837

OCTOBER

30 THURSDAY

1 FRIDAY

2 SATURDAY

3 SUNDAY

Good Marriage
– Released 10-3-2014

you feel with the neighborhood girl, that you're not exactly sure what it is, but it's there all the same. Your first kiss, and how that changes everything. One more turn in the road of many more to come. Young Bobby also has a longing for a father that isn't there, and trying to understand the overprotective mother at times. That's all here in Hicks version and done beautifully, especially with the young Anton Yelchin as Bobby. Roger Ebert's original review of the film adaptation sums it up: "The movie ends as childhood ends, in disillusionment at the real world that lies ahead." Yes, bittersweet, and the inevitable eventually arrives. I always told my kids as they were growing up, and wanted to see a horror film or other experience that I felt was still out of their reach: "you're only a kid once, so enjoy it. Soon you'll be an adult – for the rest of your life." Every single one of them understand that now. – Dave Hinchberger

SEPTEMBER

S	M	T	W	T	F	S
			1	2	3	4
5	6	7	8	9	10	11
12	13	14	15	16	17	18
19	20	21	22	23	24	25
26	27	28	29	30		

OCTOBER

S	M	T	W	T	F	S
					1	2
3	4	5	6	7	8	9
10	11	12	13	14	15	16
17	18	19	20	21	22	23
24	25	26	27	28	29	30
31						

NOVEMBER

S	M	T	W	T	F	S
	1	2	3	4	5	6
7	8	9	10	11	12	13
14	15	16	17	18	19	20
21	22	23	24	25	26	27
28	29	30				

OCTOBER

4 MONDAY

In The Tall Grass
– Released 10-4-2019

5 TUESDAY

6 WEDNESDAY

Hearts in Atlantis, Japanese DVD 2007

THE PHANTOM KNOWS

What is the name of Bobby's bike? What program is Bobby watching on the TV in his living Room? In the film, what movie is currently playing, and listed on the marquee, at The Royal Theatre? Whats the name of pool hall Ted places bets at?

Answers:

1. Black Phantom, manufactured by Schwinn from 1949 to 1959.
2. *The Lone Ranger*, which aired from 1949 to 1957 for eight seasons.
3. *Village of the Damned* is a 1960 horror science fiction film that influenced many a writer and director in these genre's over the years.
4. The Corner Pocket.

OCTOBER

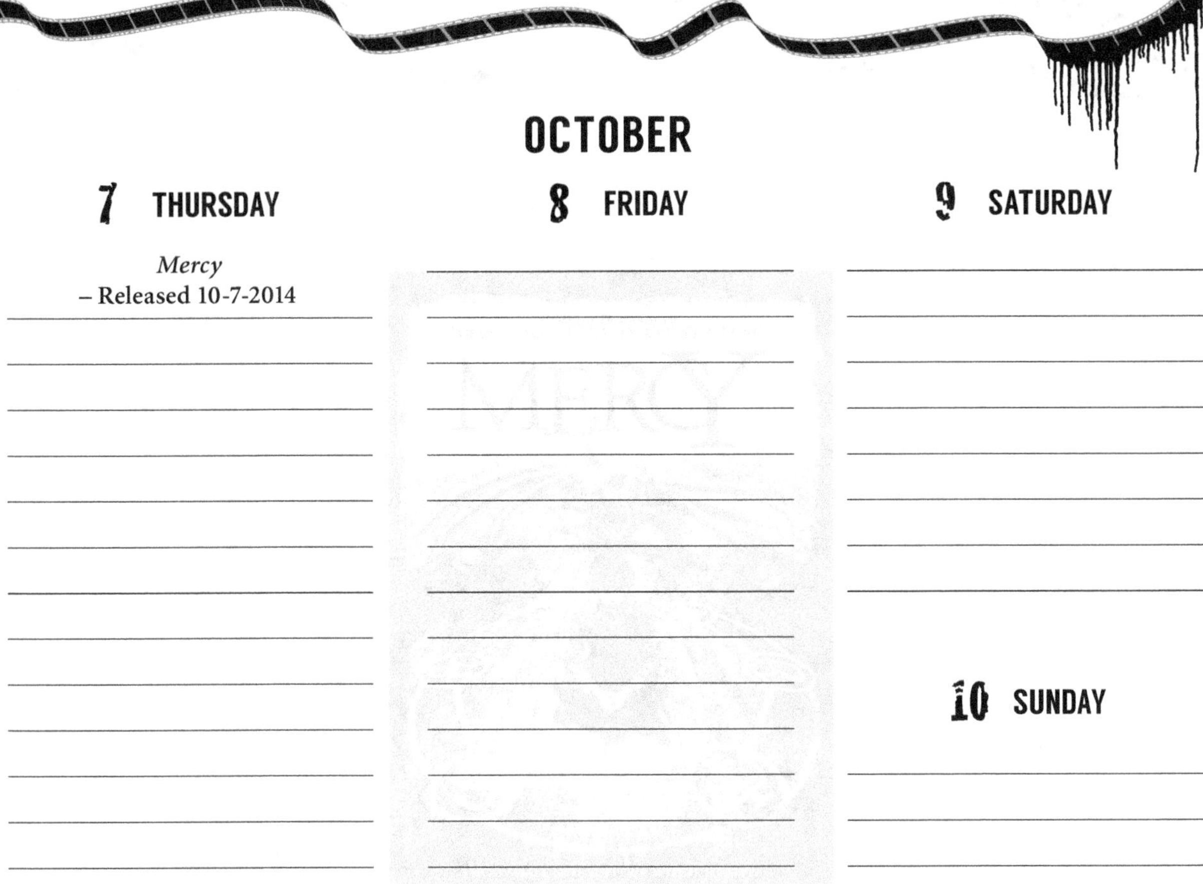

7 THURSDAY

Mercy
– Released 10-7-2014

8 FRIDAY

9 SATURDAY

10 SUNDAY

MERCY, MERCY ME.

Mercy, A 2014 film, was released direct to video in 2014. *Mercy* is loosely based on what Stephen King story? This story was originally filmed for a TV series in the 1980's. What is the name of this series? The Mercy films leading star, Chandler Riggs, became famous for what long running TV horror series? The R.L. Flag Home for the Aged is a nod for a Stephen King character. Who? What is the name of the adult diapers seen in the film, and what is this a reference too?

Answers:

1. "Gramma."
2. *The Twilight Zone*. It was resurrected and featured all new stories and creators including Stephen King's "Gramma."
3. *The Walking Dead*.
4. Randall Flagg, otherwise known as The Dark Man in *The Stand*.
5. Bachman's Ultra Comfort, is a nod to Richard Bachman, Stephen King's pseudonym for several novels including *Rage*, *The Long Walk*, and *Thinner*.

SEPTEMBER

S	M	T	W	T	F	S
			1	2	3	4
5	6	7	8	9	10	11
12	13	14	15	16	17	18
19	20	21	22	23	24	25
26	27	28	29	30		

OCTOBER

S	M	T	W	T	F	S
					1	2
3	4	5	6	7	8	9
10	11	12	13	14	15	16
17	18	19	20	21	22	23
24	25	26	27	28	29	30
31						

NOVEMBER

S	M	T	W	T	F	S
	1	2	3	4	5	6
7	8	9	10	11	12	13
14	15	16	17	18	19	20
21	22	23	24	25	26	27
28	29	30				

OCTOBER

11 MONDAY

Silver Bullet
– Released 10-11-1985

Columbus Day

12 TUESDAY

13 WEDNESDAY

Der Werewolf Von Tarker Mills is the title to the German *Silver Bullet* Blu-Ray release. This title translates to *The Werewolf From Tarker Mills.*

I SEE A BAD MOON RISING

Silver Bullet Director, Daniel Attias, has directed how many films to date? Actor Everett McGill is listed twice in the credits. Once in the beginning of the cast credits, and then as the last cast credit. For what roles (spoiler) ? What story by Stephen King is *Silver Bullet* based on? Who was the original director of *Silver Bullet*?

OCTOBER

14 THURSDAY

15 FRIDAY

Riding the Bullet
– Released 10-15-2004

16 SATURDAY

17 SUNDAY

Answers:

1. Attias has only directed one film, *Silver Bullet*. Although he was the second assistant director on many films, such as *E.T.*, *The Twilight Zone* film, and several others, he has become one of the busiest directors of TV series, as Dan Attias, in the last few decades. This includes *Castle Rock*, *True Blood*, *The Walking Dead*, *Penny Dreadful*, and over eighty productions.
2. Reverend Lowe and..(spoiler) The Werewolf.
3. Cycle of the Werewolf.
4. Don Coscarelli, the creator of the *Phantasm* movies, was originally directing the film. After filming all the non-werewolf scenes (as they waited on the werewolf suit to be completed) due to a conflict he left the project and Daniel Attias came in to complete the production.

SEPTEMBER

S	M	T	W	T	F	S
			1	2	3	4
5	6	7	8	9	10	11
12	13	14	15	16	17	18
19	20	21	22	23	24	25
26	27	28	29	30		

OCTOBER

S	M	T	W	T	F	S
					1	2
3	4	5	6	7	8	9
10	11	12	13	14	15	16
17	18	19	20	21	22	23
24	25	26	27	28	29	30
31						

NOVEMBER

S	M	T	W	T	F	S
	1	2	3	4	5	6
7	8	9	10	11	12	13
14	15	16	17	18	19	20
21	22	23	24	25	26	27
28	29	30				

OCTOBER

18 MONDAY

Carrie (2013) – Released 10-18-2013

Big Driver
– Released 10-18-2014
– TV MOVIE

19 TUESDAY

20 WEDNESDAY

1922
– Released 10-20-2017

GETTING IN... THE ZONE

Did you know there's a Simpson's homage to *The Dead Zone*? What is this episode titled? What Season / episode did it appear in? Who was Stephen King's first choice to play Johnny Smith in the film? Martin Sheen, who plays Greg Stillson running for president, did become the US President in what series? What poem does Christopher Walken, as Johnny Smith, read at the beginning of the film during the class he's teaching? *The Dead Zone* was the first story that featured a town that became prominent in many Stephen King fictions. What is the name of the town?

OCTOBER

21 THURSDAY

The Dead Zone
– Released 10-21-1983

22 FRIDAY

23 SATURDAY

Apt Pupil
– Released 10-23-1998

24 SUNDAY

Answers:

1. "The Ned Zone." Homer accidentilly hits Ned Flanders with his bowling ball and Ned wakes up in a hospital, seemingly able to predict future death and destruction. It's hilariously brilliant!
2. Season 16, Episode 1, the "Treehouse of Horror XV."
3. Bill Murray. [1]
4. *West Wing*. Oh, the irony!
5. It's the ending to "The Raven," by Edgar Allen Poe.
6. Castle Rock.

SEPTEMBER

S	M	T	W	T	F	S
			1	2	3	4
5	6	7	8	9	10	11
12	13	14	15	16	17	18
19	20	21	22	23	24	25
26	27	28	29	30		

OCTOBER

S	M	T	W	T	F	S
					1	2
3	4	5	6	7	8	9
10	11	12	13	14	15	16
17	18	19	20	21	22	23
24	25	26	27	28	29	30
31						

NOVEMBER

S	M	T	W	T	F	S
	1	2	3	4	5	6
7	8	9	10	11	12	13
14	15	16	17	18	19	20
21	22	23	24	25	26	27
28	29	30				

OCTOBER

25 MONDAY

Thinner
– Released 10-25-1996

26 TUESDAY

Graveyard Shift
– Released 10-26-1996

27 WEDNESDAY

Stephen King's *Thinner*, Japanese DVD.

GYPSY JUSTICE

Thinner was originally released under a Stephen King pseudonym. What is it? Stephen King makes a cameo in *Thinner.* What character does he play? What name is this character given? The Screenplay is by Tom Holland and… Stephen King called this writer, "The finest writer of paperback originals in America today." [1] Who is the writer? Who plays Richie Ginelli in the film. He also has another connection to *Thinner.* also narrates the audiobook of *Thinner.*

OCTOBER

28 THURSDAY

29 FRIDAY

Trucks
– Released 10-29-1997

30 SATURDAY

31 SUNDAY

Halloween

Answers:

1. Richard Bachman.
2. The Pharmacist
3. Dr. Jonathan Bangor. This is a reference to Bangor, Maine, where Stephen King resides.
4. The writer is Michael McDowell who also helped Tim Burton with screenplay and story on *Beetlejuice* and *The Nightmare Before Christmas*. *Thinner* was the last screenplay produced before his passing in 1999.
5. Joe Mantegna plays Richie Ginelli, and he also narrates the audio adaptation of *Thinner*.

SEPTEMBER

S	M	T	W	T	F	S
			1	2	3	4
5	6	7	8	9	10	11
12	13	14	15	16	17	18
19	20	21	22	23	24	25
26	27	28	29	30		

OCTOBER

S	M	T	W	T	F	S
					1	2
3	4	5	6	7	8	9
10	11	12	13	14	15	16
17	18	19	20	21	22	23
24	25	26	27	28	29	30
31						

NOVEMBER

S	M	T	W	T	F	S
	1	2	3	4	5	6
7	8	9	10	11	12	13
14	15	16	17	18	19	20
21	22	23	24	25	26	27
28	29	30				

NOVEMBER

1 MONDAY

2 TUESDAY

3 WEDNESDAY

HOW TALL IS IT?

Where was "In the Tall Grass" first published? When was it published, month and year? Who wrote this story? The poster featured here is available to purchase from Amazon. However what is wrong with this poster? Where and when did the film premiere to the world?

NOVEMBER

4 THURSDAY

5 FRIDAY

6 SATURDAY

7 SUNDAY

Daylight Savings Ends

Answers:

1. *Esquire* magazine
2. "In the Tall Grass" was published in two parts in two issues of *Esquire* magazine, date June-July double issue 2012 and August 2012. *Esquire* said in the initial press release this was the first story in their "fiction for men" series.
3. Stephen King and Joe Hill.
4. The poster only lists Stephen King, when in fact it is authored by Stephen King and his son, Joe Hill. Nice poster, but it is incorrect.
5. The film had been in development for several years but finally found a home with Netflix, the streaming service, to begin production. Netflix did release it to their subscribers on October 4, 2019 however it made it's public showing in a theater at Fantastic Fest, Austin, Texas, two weeks earlier on September 20, 2019

OCTOBER

S	M	T	W	T	F	S
					1	2
3	4	5	6	7	8	9
10	11	12	13	14	15	16
17	18	19	20	21	22	23
24	25	26	27	28	29	30
31						

NOVEMBER

S	M	T	W	T	F	S
	1	2	3	4	5	6
7	8	9	10	11	12	13
14	15	16	17	18	19	20
21	22	23	24	25	26	27
28	29	30				

DECEMBER

S	M	T	W	T	F	S
			1	2	3	4
5	6	7	8	9	10	11
12	13	14	15	16	17	18
19	20	21	22	23	24	25
26	27	28	29	30	31	

NOVEMBER

8 MONDAY

9 TUESDAY

10 WEDNESDAY

The Running Man Spanish Movie Poster. Perseguido translates to Persued.

PLEASE STAND BY:

The Running Man film is based on a novel by Stephen King under the same title. However it was released under a pseudonym of Stephen King's. What is the pseudonym? What author name is the film credited to?

Actor Richard Dawson played Damon Killian, *The Running Man* TV host. However this actor became famous for playing a real life TV game show host for a decade. Which show was it?

Two rock n' roll artists play resistance fighters in the film. Who are they?

NOVEMBER

11 THURSDAY

Veterans Day

12 FRIDAY

13 SATURDAY

The Running Man
– Released 11-13-1987

14 SUNDAY

Answers:

1. Richard Bachman.
2. Also Richard Bachman. Even though many know this is based on a pseudonymous Stephen King novel, it still eludes many others that this is indeed by Stephen King.
3. *Family Feud*. Richard Dawson was the host from 1976 to 1985.
4. Mick Fleetwood, of Fleetwood Mac, a legendary rock band.
5. Dweezil Zappa, the son of famed recording artist, record producer, filmmaker, Frank Zappa.

Juokse Tai Kuole, the Finnish video release, translates to *Run or Die*, 1990 VHS.

OCTOBER

S	M	T	W	T	F	S
					1	2
3	4	5	6	7	8	9
10	11	12	13	14	15	16
17	18	19	20	21	22	23
24	25	26	27	28	29	30
31						

NOVEMBER

S	M	T	W	T	F	S
	1	2	3	4	5	6
7	8	9	10	11	12	13
14	15	16	17	18	19	20
21	22	23	24	25	26	27
28	29	30				

DECEMBER

S	M	T	W	T	F	S
			1	2	3	4
5	6	7	8	9	10	11
12	13	14	15	16	17	18
19	20	21	22	23	24	25
26	27	28	29	30	31	

NOVEMBER

15 MONDAY

16 TUESDAY

Carrie (1976)
– Released 11-16-1976

17 WEDNESDAY

DID YOU KNOW? Sissy Spacek was the Senior Year Homecoming Queen at Texas's Quitman High School in 1968. No joke. I bet her first class reunion was a lot of fun. While attending a book event in Ft. Myers, Florida, in 2010 Stephen King discussed how he was paid just $2,500 for the movie rights to *Carrie*. Considering the success he's had with films since then this amount is quite low. However King was quick to point out "I was fortunate to have that happen to my first book," King said [1]. Not only was he fortunate to have a film but it was a huge hit. After a 1.8 million investment it went on to make over 33 million at the box office. *Carrie* was the first film to have duplicate scenes shot. One for theatrical release and a cleaned up version for TV. There are apparently several versions of this cleaned up release out there but aren't as easy to discover now.

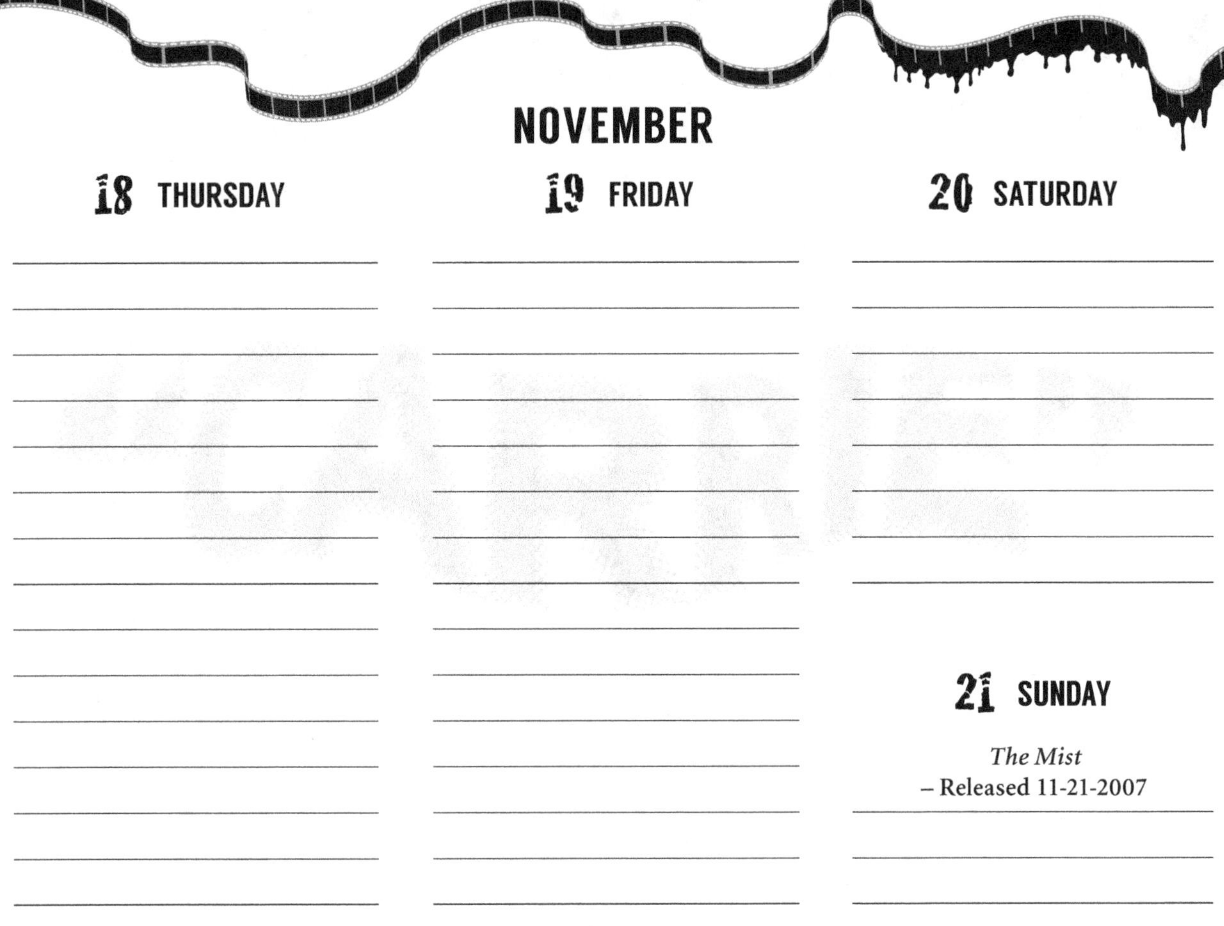

NOVEMBER

18 THURSDAY

19 FRIDAY

20 SATURDAY

21 SUNDAY

The Mist
– Released 11-21-2007

HIGH SCHOOL HIGH JINX

What is the name of Carrie's high school in the film? What is it in the book? Who is the screenwriter of *Carrie*? What other Stephen King productions is he associated with?

Answers:

1. Bates High School, as a tribute to Norman Bates from Psycho.
2. Ewen High School.
3. Lawrence D. Cohen. Mr. Cohen championed the *Carrie* script from the first time he read the original version in May 1973. He later was able to create a truer version of the novel into a new script and the rest, as they say, is history.
4. Mr Cohen also wrote Part 1 of the 1990 TV film of *IT*, Part 1 and 2 of *The Tommyknockers* TV film, and "The End of the Whole Mess" for the *Nightmares & Dreamscapes* TV series.

Carrie Blu-Ray Collector's Edition, 2016 Shout Factory. See more of screenwriter, Lawrence D. Cohen's interviews on his long association with Carrie since 1973.

OCTOBER

S	M	T	W	T	F	S
					1	2
3	4	5	6	7	8	9
10	11	12	13	14	15	16
17	18	19	20	21	22	23
24	25	26	27	28	29	30
31						

NOVEMBER

S	M	T	W	T	F	S
	1	2	3	4	5	6
7	8	9	10	11	12	13
14	15	16	17	18	19	20
21	22	23	24	25	26	27
28	29	30				

DECEMBER

S	M	T	W	T	F	S
			1	2	3	4
5	6	7	8	9	10	11
12	13	14	15	16	17	18
19	20	21	22	23	24	25
26	27	28	29	30	31	

NOVEMBER

22 MONDAY

23 TUESDAY

24 WEDNESDAY

A MOMENT ON THE MILE No.1: TOM HANKS BATHROOM

Director Frank Darabont had been a customer of our store The Overlook Connection Bookstore (the parent store for StephenKingCatalog.com) for years. I knew he was going to be filming *The Green Mile* in Tennessee and Frank graciously let me visit the set. Since I live in Atlanta, about four hours away, I carved out some time to visit the set for a couple of days. Not an easy task when you're running a bookstore and a press. As any entrepreneur will tell you, you work *all* the time, so time away is a luxury. However this was a chance of a lifetime to see Frank in action, and to see in person Stephen King's wonderful story being filmed. So I hauled myself up to Nashville for a couple of days. Frank told me where he, Tom Hanks, and the cast were staying so I booked a room there for a couple of nights. The next morning I headed out with directions in hand, eager to get to my moment on the *Mile*. I hadn't realized how far this was, GPS wasn't common in 1998, and this became a longer drive than I'd expected. It was an hour away, south… in the middle of nowhere Tennessee. After traveling many miles to get to the *Mile* – the freeway, a highway, back roads, and now a dirt road, I'd arrived at my destination. I'd

NOVEMBER

25 THURSDAY

Thanksgiving Day

26 FRIDAY

27 SATURDAY

28 SUNDAY

lived in areas like this when I was growing up in south Georgia. It's a different world of large fields along dirt roads, homes of various makes, sizes and looks. Wide open spaces that makes you feel like the world is yours to explore, feeling free. Today's location was the country house scene in the film where Tom Hanks and Gary Sinise are on the back porch discussing the complexities of Hanks' prisoner, John Coffey. It's a long scene, about six non-stop minutes when filming, if I remember correctly. When I first walked up… quietly… as Frank was working, directing the scene, I just held back and watched the cast, crew, and director filming their magic. When Frank had a break I was able to meet

Milagros Inesperados is *The Green Mile* Spanish DVD. The title translates to *Unexpected Miracles.*

OCTOBER

S	M	T	W	T	F	S
					1	2
3	4	5	6	7	8	9
10	11	12	13	14	15	16
17	18	19	20	21	22	23
24	25	26	27	28	29	30
31						

NOVEMBER

S	M	T	W	T	F	S
	1	2	3	4	5	6
7	8	9	10	11	12	13
14	15	16	17	18	19	20
21	22	23	24	25	26	27
28	29	30				

DECEMBER

S	M	T	W	T	F	S
			1	2	3	4
5	6	7	8	9	10	11
12	13	14	15	16	17	18
19	20	21	22	23	24	25
26	27	28	29	30	31	

NOVEMBER

29 MONDAY

First Day of Hanukkah

30 TUESDAY

Misery
– Released 11-30-1990

1 WEDNESDAY

him for the first time. After all these years on the phone, it was good to finally meet the man in person. I gave him a big ol' Dave hug and thanked him for allowing me to visit during his busy schedule. He was wearing a baseball jacket, a baseball cap, and had the biggest smile when we met. For me it was a grand moment. I've always appreciated his work and now I was here, able to watch him create in person. After watching the back porch scene, over and over again, I decided to walk around and see what was out here on this scenic location. You see this was being filmed at a *real* house, occupied by a *real* family (although they stayed somewhere else during filming), and it was leased out by the movie production. This wasn't just a house, it was a farm, with fields, with animals, in the barn, kicking, clucking and mooing. I decided to take a look within as there

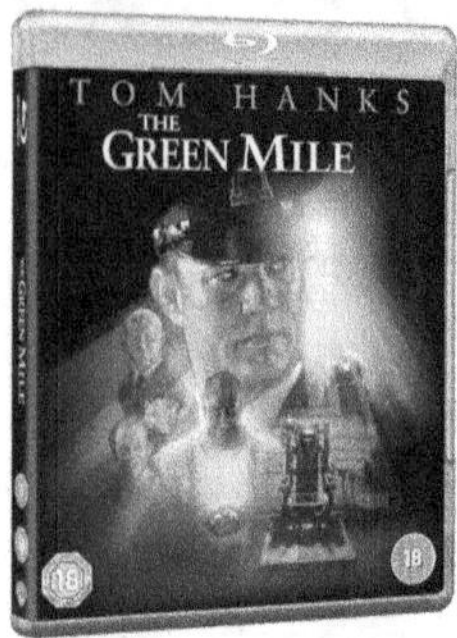

was an unusual structure smack dab in the middle of the barns walkway… a bathroom. A bathroom that was constructed for *The Green Mile*. Not for the cast, or the crew, or visitors such as myself, it was created for, well, the film's star, Tom Hanks. On the inside it looked like it had brick walls, with old green paint, chips here and there, like it had been painted over many times through the years. A medicine cabinet – with fabricated old medicines inside! The toilet had a pull chain above. The whole bathroom was something you'd have used earlier in the century. Except this bathroom was sitting *inside* this barn, and not part of any structure. The stalls, lining either side of the barn,

DECEMBER

2 THURSDAY

3 FRIDAY

4 SATURDAY

5 SUNDAY

housed horses and cows. Chickens were running around. There was straw strewn about on the dirt floor. The outside of the bathroom had hundreds of nails sticking out of it, all new materials of wood and the like. You'd never imagine there was an old prison bathroom within this structure from the outside. I asked Frank's assistant at the time, Dave Johnson (who's become a successful screenwriter himself, with *Orphan*, and several others. Look him up!), "what's the bathroom for?" He said "it might rain today and tomorrow and if we can't film this outside scene with Tom we're going to film him for the prison pissing scene." I said, with eye brows raised, "in the... barn?" He nodded and grinned in response seeing the surprise on my face. "Let me get this straight, they built a bathroom as a back up. What if you don't need it, will they use this again somewhere else?" Dave Johnson said "If we don't use the bathroom, it will probably go to the dump. A real version of the bathroom is back at the prison location and we'll just film it there. This is just a backup so we don't waste time." This is when it struck me just how much money Hollywood spends on production. They'll create a bathroom, a *backup bathroom*, just in case. As Tom Hanks was being paid 20 million for *The Green Mile*, then I guess you make sure you certainly don't waste *any* time. If you think about it in that way, the bathroom was cheap insurance for a sixty million dollar film, or rather... the Twenty Million Dollar Man.

DECEMBER

6 MONDAY

Last Day of Hanukkah

7 TUESDAY

8 WEDNESDAY

ASSEMBLY BY HITCHCOCK.

"...we did this as an idea that Alfred Hitchcock had come up with a long time ago, he thought it would be great to have a scene where you watch a car being assembled from nothing, beginning to the end, and at the very end of the assembly line a body falls out of the trunk. So it seemed kind of appropriate. We didn't show it put together but I got to do a little bit of an assembly line, and I got to show off the car. I don't remember how many cars we had, there were a lot, but I remember we destroyed a lot of them." - John Carpenter on the early film scene where Christine is coming down the assembly line and as the car stops someone opens the drivers side door and man falls out onto the floor. Dead.

"I just remember the surreal beauty of walking into this warehouse where we were shooting the film, and there were like twenty or so of the cars lined up perfectly next to each other...just like a showroom of Christine's." - Keith Gordon, actor who played Arnie in *Christine*.

DECEMBER

9 THURSDAY

Christine
– Released 12-9-1983

10 FRIDAY

The Green Mile
– Released 12-10-1999

11 SATURDAY

12 SUNDAY

SUMMER DRIVE IN TRIVIA

During the Drive-In theater scene with Dennis and Leigh, and of course, Christine, the film playing on the big screen was a 70's hit. What is the name of this film? Who is the female actress in this scene?

Answers:

Thank God it's Friday. This film, released during the disco dance craze of the late 70's, featured popular disco singer, Dronna Summer as an up and coming singer trying to get the DJ to play her record for this popular night club in Los Angeles. Donna Summer won the Academy Award® for Best Original Song for „Last Dance."

Christine Columbia Pictures DVD Special Edition, 2004

NOVEMBER

S	M	T	W	T	F	S
	1	2	3	4	5	6
7	8	9	10	11	12	13
14	15	16	17	18	19	20
21	22	23	24	25	26	27
28	29	30				

DECEMBER

S	M	T	W	T	F	S
			1	2	3	4
5	6	7	8	9	10	11
12	13	14	15	16	17	18
19	20	21	22	23	24	25
26	27	28	29	30	31	

JANUARY

S	M	T	W	T	F	S
						1
2	3	4	5	6	7	8
9	10	11	12	13	14	15
16	17	18	19	20	21	22
23	24	25	26	27	28	29
30	31					

DECEMBER

13 MONDAY

14 TUESDAY

15 WEDNESDAY

RAT TRAP *1922* is an original novella by Stephen King. What collection was it published in? Thomas Jane, the lead actor who plays Wilfred Leland James in *1922*, has also appeared in two more Stephen King adaptations. Name them. The James family lives in Hemingford Home, Nebraska, which is also the home to another Stephen King character. Who is this character? Which novel do they appear in?

Answers:

1. *Full Dark, No Stars.*
2. *The Mist* and *Dreamcatcher.*
3. "Mother Abagail" Freemantle
4. The Stand, by Stephen King.

DECEMBER

16 THURSDAY

17 FRIDAY

18 SATURDAY

19 SUNDAY

"The guy has an uncanny ability to tap into the dark side of what it means to be human and he does it in a way that feels real." – Thomas Jane on Stephen King.[1] Thomas Jane should have an idea about Stephen King's work at this point in his career. He's had successful roles in three Stephen King film adaptations. His first was as Dr. Henry Devlin in *Dreamcatcher* (2003), then as David Drayton, a father trying to protect his son in *The Mist* (2007). However it's his impressive turn as Wilfred James in *1922* (2017) that has brought this actor considerable critical, and viewer, acclaim. I believe a lot of this performance can be attributed to Jane spending time trying to get the James character right. He worked with a vocal coach to research the "dialectic idiosyncrasies of Nebraskans in the 1920s, called on summers spent growing up in Alabama to keep Wilfred from turning into a stock southern simpleton, and ended up channeling his own grandfather." [2] Oh, and the rats. They worked with real rats. As Thomas Jane so aptly puts it, "We couldn't afford no fake rats." (fake being CGI creations)

DECEMBER

20 MONDAY

21 TUESDAY

22 WEDNESDAY

APT PUPIL – TEXT TO SCREAMPLAY!

As with most film adaptations there will be differences from the author's original vision to the filmmakers final production of it on the big screen. A filmmaker's job is to try and convey the author's original story to the screen. This isn't as easy as you might think, dear reader. Yes, we all have our own mind movie version of a story, this is what makes Stephen King so relatable to his readers: we can easily see what he's conveying to us in words. Now try reversing that idea by seeing it through someone else's screenplay idea of the same story. Doesn't always fit what we

imagine. Bring in the director, producers, and anyone who pulls the purse strings. They may want it to fit a certain time frame for budgetary reasons, both during production, and profits from the theater. The final result can be a mangled idea of what you had originally read. For those filmmakers that do pull off something close to the author's original idea, well, that's cinemagic as far as I'm concerned. At this point if you haven't seen the film (or read the book) you may want to skip this section full of spoilers. So let's take a look changes with *Apt Pupil*, from book to the 1998 screenplay. The original novella has Todd Bowden in junior high in 1974 until graduation. The film takes place in 1984 during his senior year of high school. The novella has three years of meeting up with Nazi Dussander, learning his story and transferring these experiences in committing his own murders of transients and

DECEMBER

23 THURSDAY

24 FRIDAY

Christmas Eve

25 SATURDAY

Christmas Day

26 SUNDAY

homeless. The film has Dussander's attempt to kill a homeless man he's brought home, only to have Todd come and help complete the job and bury the evidence. The novella had animosity towards Jews with Dussander, but in the film this was toned down some. The novella has a dream sequence that has Todd raping a teenage Jewish virgin, with Dussander cheering him on in a Nazi laboratory. In it's place the film uses a dream sequence with Todd taking a shower that he then becomes aware he's in a gas chamber. Todd's get together with Betty in the novella also turned into dreams of torturing and raping her in a concentration camp. The film has her name as Becky where during a drive-in date he finds he's unable to perform sexually. Director Bryan Singer reduced the violence from the text trying not to make it "exploitative or repetitive."[1] Todd's school counselor discovers that Dussander is not Todd's grandfather and approaches the boy about this information. Bowden murders the counselor to silence the secret. Todd then goes on a shooting spree eventually ending in his own death. For the film the director felt he couldn't accomplish this: "I told Stephen King the ending reads so beautifully. I could never measure up to it; I would have killed it."[2]. In the film Todd blackmails the counselor by threats of rumor that would have cost him job and family. Stanley Wiater, co-author of *The Complete Stephen King Universe*, wrote, "As depicted on screen, Todd is much more consciously evil, in his way, than in the book. This switch, while making the ending less brutal, perhaps, achieves the impossible: it also makes the ending even darker."

Apt Pupil German Movie Poster. *Der Musterschüler* translates into *The Model Student.*

DECEMBER

27 MONDAY

28 TUESDAY

29 WEDNESDAY

"Any good marriage is secret territory, a necessary white space on society's map. What others don't know about it is what makes it yours." – Stephen King

Stephen King has said publicly in many interviews that he based *A Good Marriage* on the BTK Killer, Dennis Rader. Rader was convicted as a serial killer in 2005 and his wife of 34 years claimed to have no knowledge of his killings or unusual behavior. "I wanted to explore the idea that most people are sleeping with a stranger," says King, who's been married for 43 years.[1] "She never had a clue of what he was doing and this secret life that he had, and so I started to think, I wonder how many of us are sleeping with strangers and what we really know about the people that we think we're close to." [2] This is also Stephen King's first screenplay since he penned the 1989 film version of *Pet Sematary.*

DECEMBER

30 THURSDAY

31 FRIDAY
New Year's Eve

1 SATURDAY
New Year's Day

2 SUNDAY

SLEEPY HOLLOW'S KINGLY VISIT

"Stephen King and Sleepy Hollow were made for each other," said Anthony Giaccio, Sleepy Hollow Village Administrator. A good marriage, if you will.[1] "With his macabre stories ... it makes sense to have him here." The film company is using a Dutch colonial house in Sleepy Hollow (owned by the Historic Hudson Valley) that had major renovations and was refurbished, outfitting it with new floors, cabinets, etc., and painting the outside. It was all updated for a 15-day shoot for the Stephen King film *A Good Marriage*. The house, located at 429 Bellwood Avenue, was used for the film from the end of May into June, 2013. The village itself received about $1,000 a day for police details during filming, and naturally boosted the local economy and used local contractors for the work. Sleepy Hollow has had a previous King connection: The Ramones actually filmed the video for Stephen King's film *Pet Sematary* in Sleepy Hollow Cemetery itself, back in 1989. As Washining Irving, who wrote "The Legend of Sleepy Hollow," and who is also buried there, has continued an extensive legend of it's own. "Perhaps most importantly, Sleepy Hollow will add to its impressive resume that a Stephen King movie was filmed here," said spokesman Rob Schweitzer. "How great is that for the Halloween capital of America?"[2]

Couple Modele translates to *Model Couple* for the French DVD version of *A Good Marriage*.

NOVEMBER

S	M	T	W	T	F	S
	1	2	3	4	5	6
7	8	9	10	11	12	13
14	15	16	17	18	19	20
21	22	23	24	25	26	27
28	29	30				

DECEMBER

S	M	T	W	T	F	S
			1	2	3	4
5	6	7	8	9	10	11
12	13	14	15	16	17	18
19	20	21	22	23	24	25
26	27	28	29	30	31	

JANUARY

S	M	T	W	T	F	S
						1
2	3	4	5	6	7	8
9	10	11	12	13	14	15
16	17	18	19	20	21	22
23	24	25	26	27	28	29
30	31					

JANUARY

3 MONDAY | **4 TUESDAY** | **5 WEDNESDAY**

THE LOST STEPHEN KING FILM...

Director Alan Bridges, originally from Liverpool, had been producing UK TV and film for decades, and had success in the 1980's with his film *The Shooting Party*, starring James Mason, Edward Fox and John Gielgud. After *The Shooting Party* he left for America, where he began the production of an adaptation of Stephen King's novella *Apt Pupil*, in which an American teenager discovers his elderly German neighbor is a Nazi war criminal. He'd offered the Nazi neighbor role to his previous star, James Mason, but then he passed away from a heart attack before production. He then offered it to Richard Burton, who was considering the role when he then suddenly died as well. Alan Bridges did find his man for the role with Scottish actor Nicol Williamson as the Nazi and Ricky Schroder as his pupil. They had forty minutes of finished film completed, with only ten days left to finish, when the checks started bouncing. The money had abruptly run out. The film shoot halted and was never finished. The film had a budget of fourteen million, but ran out at nine million spent. Although I think the actor choices were good, especially with Nicol Williamson, it was definitely a dark turn at acting for Ricky Schroder.

JANUARY

6 THURSDAY

7 FRIDAY

8 SATURDAY

9 SUNDAY

He'd gained popular status as Ricky Stratten, the cute young man in the 80's family comedy, *Silver Spoons*. As an actor I'm sure this would have shown he could shrug that wholesome image with the young sociopath, Todd Bowden, in *Apt Pupil*. Will we ever get to see this footage? Probably not… unless… a streaming site were to offer up uncompleted pilots, films, etc. to an audience of film lovers who wanted to see these productions. I would sign up in an instant! However contractual obligations, actors who feel it doesn't represent completed work, et el, would probably halt such an idea. Never say never as time will tell. Either way, we'll never get to see a completed production of the original *Apt Pupil*, for them, and for us, it's the only time I wish school hadn't ended early.

Apt Pupil, Haven Bound edition cover art. Limited to 150 copies and signed by artist, Glenn Chadbourne. Available at StephenKingCatalog.com

DECEMBER

S	M	T	W	T	F	S
			1	2	3	4
5	6	7	8	9	10	11
12	13	14	15	16	17	18
19	20	21	22	23	24	25
26	27	28	29	30	31	

JANUARY

S	M	T	W	T	F	S
						1
2	3	4	5	6	7	8
9	10	11	12	13	14	15
16	17	18	19	20	21	22
23	24	25	26	27	28	29
30	31					

FEBRUARY

S	M	T	W	T	F	S
		1	2	3	4	5
6	7	8	9	10	11	12
13	14	15	16	17	18	19
20	21	22	23	24	25	26
27	28					

JANUARY

10 MONDAY

11 TUESDAY

12 WEDNESDAY

GET A LEG UP!

The *Misery* movie prop leg from the infamous "hobbling scene." A movie prop collector wanted to get a recreation of this scene. So they hired Tom Spina Creations for the job. Based on *Misery*, by Stephen King, which tells the story of a famous author played by James Caan, who ends up a captive of his "number 1 fan" played by Kathy Bates. In one of the most infamous scenes in all of horror history, she tries to stop him from escaping by breaking both of his legs. Since they obviously couldn't just start swinging a sledgehammer at James Caan's leg they created a silicone leg that could be hit. They spent a lot of time finding the proper style of rope for the bed, the correct bed frame, the right sort of sledgehammer (lightweight foam prop), the sweat pants, the color of the wood stain, etc. Referencing the scene, over and over again, photos from the shoot, to make it as exact as possible. They weren't able to match the sheets but as the client is also an artist they actually custom hand painted the sheets so they were a perfect replica to the screen used set! The final display is sliced right out of the film scene and just looking at this movie prop makes you go, "ouch!"

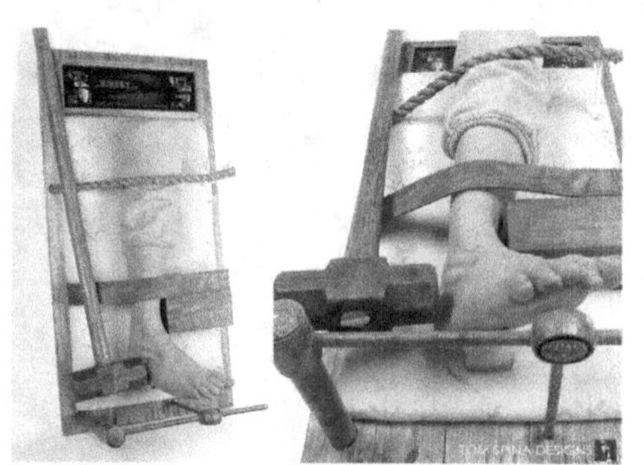

Courtesy of Tom Spina at **TomSpinaDesigns.com**

Tom Spina and crew are a source for original film prop conservation, restoration and display, along with the creation of custom sculpture and characters. Their clients include most of the major Hollywood studios. You can discover more about them at tomspinadesigns.com

JANUARY

13 THURSDAY

14 FRIDAY

15 SATURDAY

16 SUNDAY

DID YOU KNOW?

Screenwriter William Goldman wrote in his non-fiction collection of Hollywood stories, *What Lie Did I tell?* that the part of Paul Sheldon was originally offered to many others before James Caan. In fact it was indeed a who's who of talent: William Hurt (twice), Kevin Kline, Michael Douglas, Harrison Ford, Dustin Hoffman, Robert De Niro, Al Pacino, Richard Dreyfuss, Gene Hackman, and Robert Redford. They all turned down the role. [1] Warren Beatty was interested but had a conflict with the extended filming of *Dick Tracy*. Eventually someone suggested James Caan, who agreed to play the part. Caan commented that he was attracted by how Sheldon was a role unlike any other of his, and that "being a totally reactionary character is really much tougher."[2] According to director Rob Reiner, it was William Goldman who suggested that Kathy Bates, then unknown, should portray Annie Wilkes. Of course Kathy Bates would go on to win the Academy Award® for Actress in a Leading Role in Misery. Within her speech she said: "I would like to thank Jimmy Caan, and apologize publicly for the ankles."
Now if she had given him a gold topped cane, now that would have been an apology.

A Misery placard used on the movie set to identify vehicles, which will be placed on car dashboards, and / or posted in areas that were used for filming in various locations. Castlerock Productions.

JANUARY

17 MONDAY

Martin Luther King, Jr. Day

18 TUESDAY

19 WEDNESDAY

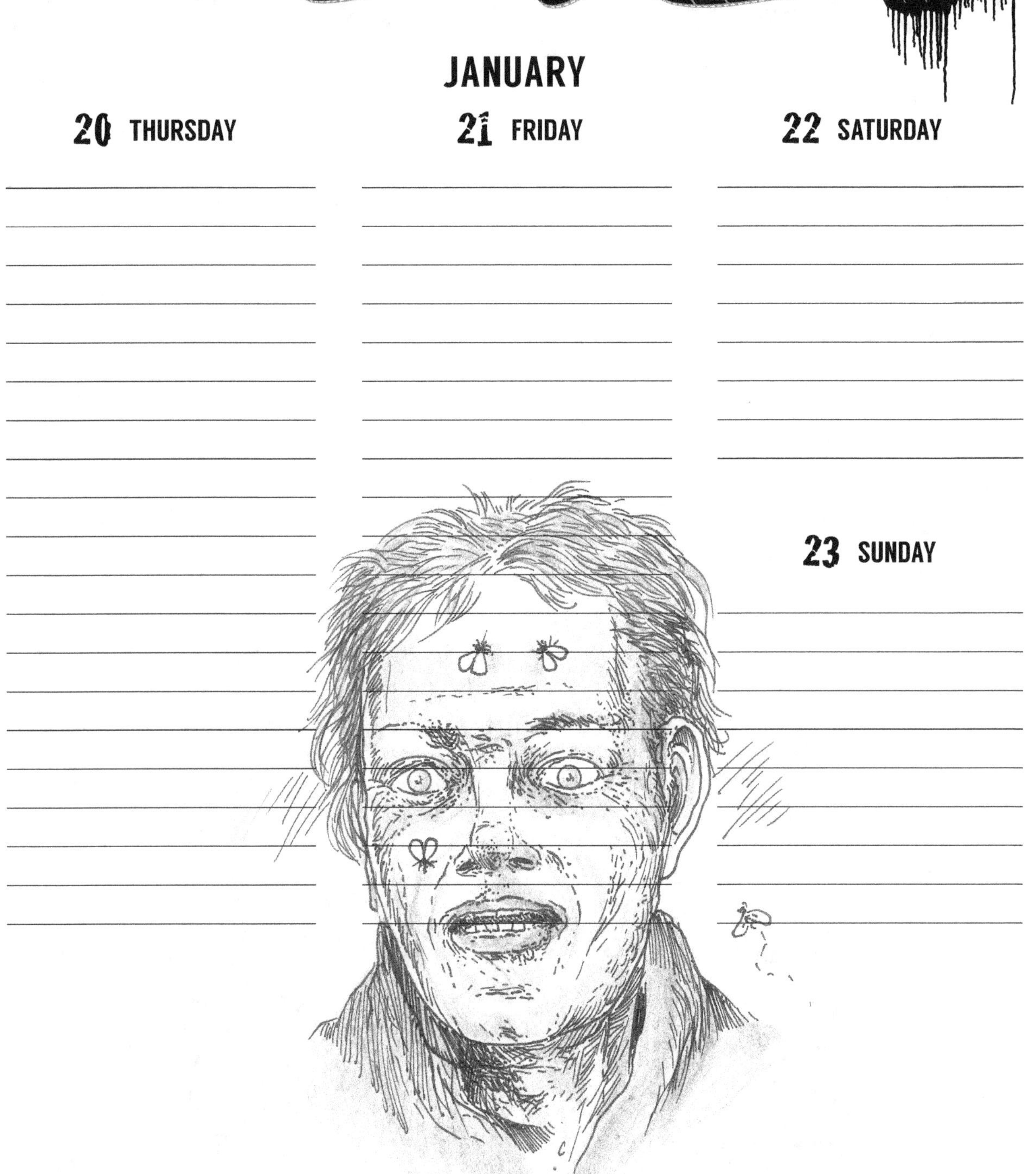

JANUARY

20 THURSDAY

21 FRIDAY

22 SATURDAY

23 SUNDAY

DECEMBER

S	M	T	W	T	F	S
			1	2	3	4
5	6	7	8	9	10	11
12	13	14	15	16	17	18
19	20	21	22	23	24	25
26	27	28	29	30	31	

JANUARY

S	M	T	W	T	F	S
						1
2	3	4	5	6	7	8
9	10	11	12	13	14	15
16	17	18	19	20	21	22
23	24	25	26	27	28	29
30	31					

FEBRUARY

S	M	T	W	T	F	S
		1	2	3	4	5
6	7	8	9	10	11	12
13	14	15	16	17	18	19
20	21	22	23	24	25	26
27	28					

JANUARY

24 MONDAY

25 TUESDAY

26 WEDNESDAY

JANUARY

27 THURSDAY

28 FRIDAY

29 SATURDAY

30 SUNDAY

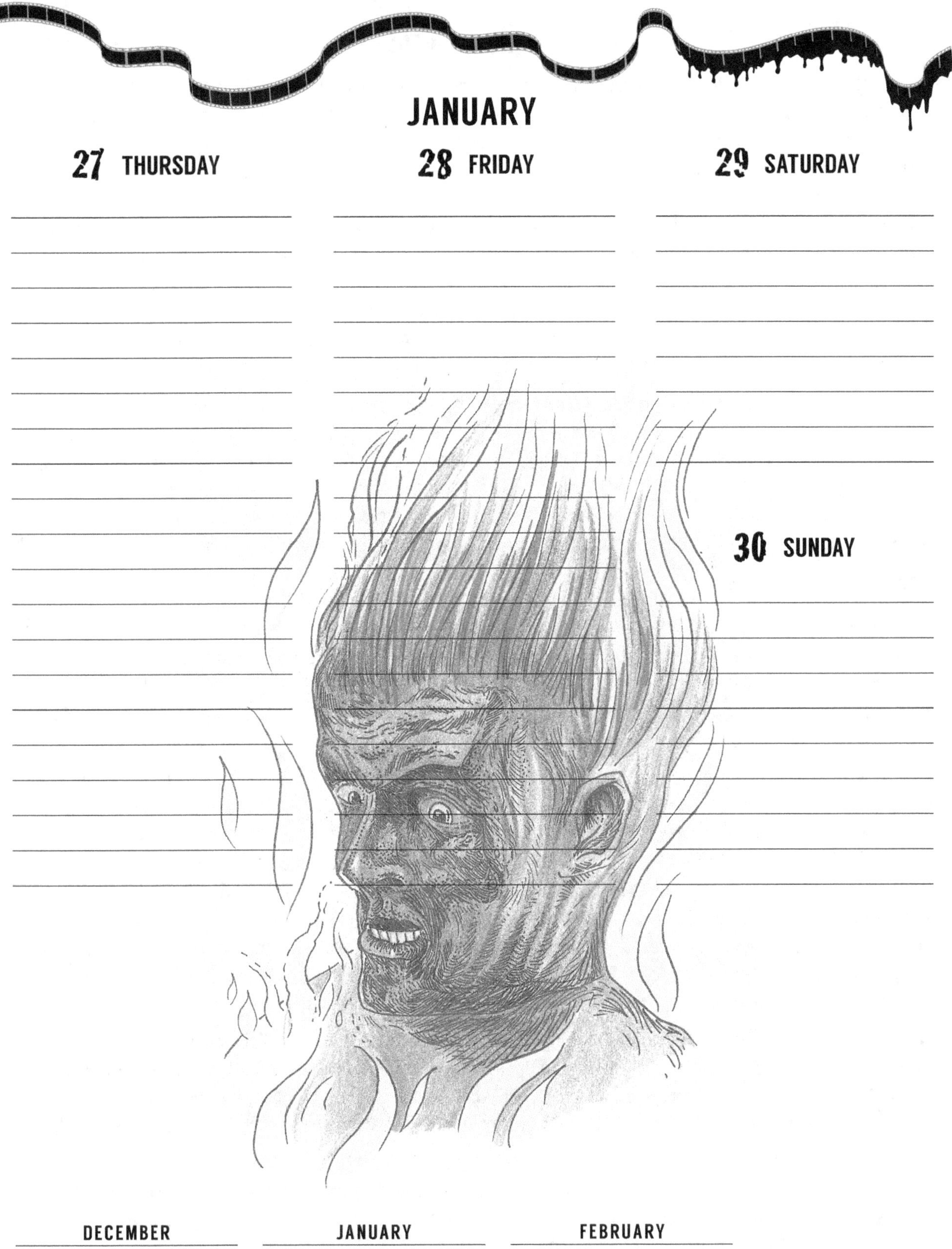

DECEMBER

S	M	T	W	T	F	S
			1	2	3	4
5	6	7	8	9	10	11
12	13	14	15	16	17	18
19	20	21	22	23	24	25
26	27	28	29	30	31	

JANUARY

S	M	T	W	T	F	S
						1
2	3	4	5	6	7	8
9	10	11	12	13	14	15
16	17	18	19	20	21	22
23	24	25	26	27	28	29
30	31					

FEBRUARY

S	M	T	W	T	F	S
		1	2	3	4	5
6	7	8	9	10	11	12
13	14	15	16	17	18	19
20	21	22	23	24	25	26
27	28					

CONTRIBUTORS:

Dave Hinchberger – I devour everything. Whether it's movies or comic books, novels or theater, Rock n' Roll to Jazz. Before I was in "books" I managed record stores and was in charge of marketing at Polygram and Relativity Records for over a decade. Lots of stories, and more importantly, lots of great music. During the growing up years if we weren't listening to the Beatles, then at night I'd be tuning into the *CBS Mystery Theater* on the car radio. Traveling late at night with my family on long car trips. All of my brothers, and sister, huddled in behind mom and dad in the Country Squire station wagon, as the fateful sound of the drum roll theme came echoing out of the tinny car speakers. Hairs raised on our necks. Experiencing *Planet of the Apes* in the theater with my dad, at the age of six, which really showed me what horror could have in store for us. Funny enough, it also intrigued me. At ten I stumbled upon Jack Kirby's *Kamandi: The Last Boy on Earth*. Kirby really impressed this young man, living off a dirt road, in the wilds of southern Georgia, where imagination can run free. I've been operating The Overlook Connection Bookstore and Press, since 1987, and then created The Stephen King Catalog to dedicate this area to everything Stephen King.

Glenn Chadbourne – This amazing artist is well known in the horror world of writers, artists, and even in film (if you look close in Stephen King's *The Mist*, directed by Frank Darabont, you'll see Glenn's work). Artist to the stars, we all call him. Illustrator of so many novels and short story collections, but especially Stephen King special editions. Too many to mention here, but he did create a beautiful two-volume set, *The Secretary of Dreams*, an illustrated short story collection that spans some of King's best short fiction. This project took him years to complete, and it was well worth the wait. Glenn is also the artist for the New Stephen King Cover Series that gives every Stephen King book a new cover and he's about half way there (see ad in this calendar). Of course his work covers this calendar, and is scarily placed throughout this year. Glenn frequently visits a beach near his home in Maine. A place he calls, "Pumpkin Cove." We spent some time down at the Cove with him. This little place is a beach with lots of rocks, not sand mind you, and dark forests that hang to the left and right of this dark water bay. I wouldn't want to be caught alone there at night, but you do get a feel of the world of "Uncle Glenny." You can see a whole category with hundreds of items from Glenn Chadbourne at **StephenKingCatalog.com** and at **glennchadbourne.com**.

Bryan McAllister – Bryan has been helping bring OCP projects to life since 2002. A sci-fi fan from early on he honed his art abilities after seeing Star Wars and emulating their gorgeous craftsmanship. He's the man behind the graphic design and illustration studio, Fine Dog Creative. He's also a caver. After an eventful cave trip with his father in his youth, he now belongs to a local caving club. He's helped discover new underground caves, as well as mapping and surveying them. He serves on the board of directors of the MCKC (Missouri Cave and Karst Conservancy) and is a Life Member of the NSS (National Speleological Society)and was awarded their title of Fellow in 2016. The "eventful" story has a lot to do with *The Land of the Lost* TV series from the 70's and the scares within! The moral of the story? Conquer those fears, whatever they be! His *Cujo* contribution within brings the heat we all felt with that story by Stephen King and is a moment in time I'm glad he shared with us here. Bryan lives in St. Louis with his lovely wife, Laura, and their two children and Maya the wonder dog.

Anthony Northrup is a two-time award winning writer who had been a contributor to his local newspaper, The Tri County Sun for 8yrs and a contributor to International web page Through the Black Hole for 8yrs. He is also the creator and head writer of ATK - All Things King- a Stephen King fanpage for 8yrs. He has been a contributor to two Stephen Spignesi books: *Stephen King American Master* and *Elton John Fifty Years On*. His new book, *Stephen King Dollar Baby*, will be available early 2021. He currently lives in North Dakota with his wife Gena.

Brian Skutle is a film critic and podcaster who runs his own website, Sonic Cinema. Brian's main point of interest is film analysis and criticism and filmmaker interviews, which are the focus of his podcast, the Sonic Cinema Podcast, which is available on Apple, Google and Spotify. Among his favorite Stephen King movies are *The Shining*, *Creepshow*, *The Mist*, *Stand by Me*, and the *IT* movies. You can visit his website at: **www.sonic-cinema.com**

Tyson Blue, one of the first-generation Stephen King scholars, has written and published thousands of essays, reviews, interviews, books and articles about Stephen King and his work. His latest, *Hope and Miracles: The Shawshank Redemption and The Green Mile: Two Screenplays by Frank Darabont*, is coming in November 2020 from Gauntlet Press.

Apt Pupil

The Mist

Haven Bound Editions

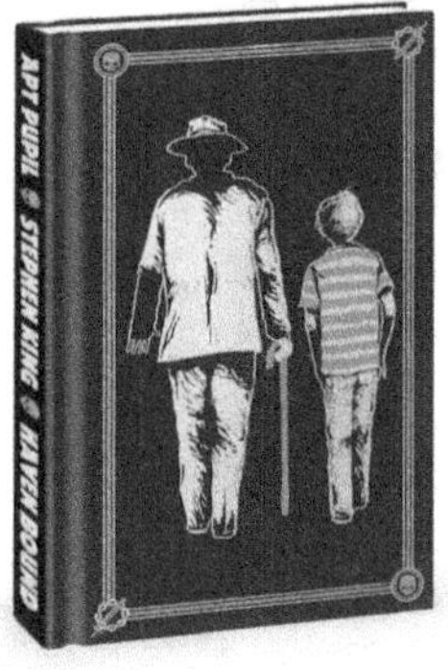

Apt Pupil fvoil stamping

Haven Bound editions are bindings of new and out of print Stephen King titles. Each release is selected with the idea of offering a first ever hardcover of a release as well as bringing back the magnificence of a title with special cloth and / or leather bindings. Featuring original foil stamped artwork on the front, spine and back of each edition. Some editions feature original cover and endpaper artwork by the preeminent artist in the Stephen King world, Glenn Chadbourne.

Every edition is bound with unique features and vary in signed artist and numbered print runs.

Cycle of the Werewolf

Features Include:

~ **Each binding features a bound in silk book marker.**
~ **Signed on the front end paper by artist, Glenn Chadbourne.**
~ **Each copy features a foil embossed stamp with the limitation number.**
~ **Each release features a unique binding of cloth and / or leather.**
~ **A portion of sales is donated to Stephen King's Haven Foundation for artists and authors in need.**

Current and upcoming titles include: *Later, Apt Pupil, Cycle of the Werewolf, The Sun Dog, Rita Hayworth and the Shawshank Redemption, The Mist, Creepshow, Joyland*, et el.

Visit **StephenKingCatalog.com** and search for **Haven** to see all titles

Stephen King Catalog is a subsidiary of The Overlook Connection Bookstore and Press, since 1987.
Specializing in Stephen King, Horror, Science Fiction, Fantasy and Mystery.
Signed limiteds, Special Editions, Video, Audio, Ephemera, et el.

PO Box 1934 Hiram Georgia 30141
StephenKingCatalog.com ~ OverlookConnection.com ~ ServiceOverlook@gmail.com

BIBLIOGRAPHY

PG 1. Glenn Chadbourne. Limited edition print of 250 copies for Cemetery Dance publications.

PG 2. Dave Hinchberger. "Welcome Back My Friends to the Show That Never Ends." 2021 Calendar Introduction.

PG 2. Glenn Chadbourne, zombie portrait of Dave Hinchberger, 2017.

PG 4,5. *Riding the Bullet* Artwork, 2010 Lonely Roads Press, Mick Garris.

PG 4. Mick Garris. *Riding the Bullet*: A Screenplay, 2010 Lonely Roads Press.

PG 5. Dave Hinchberger, "Getting Graphic." 2020. Original.

PG 6,7. Dave Hinchberger, "In Name Only." 2020. Original.

PG 6,7. *Lawnmower Man* Artists Edition Portfolio. IDW, 2014. Artwork by Walter Simonson.

PG 10. "Shining Inspiration," Dave Hinchberger. 2020. Original.

PG 11. "Let Morton Reign," Dave Hinchberger. 2020. Original.

PG 12,13. *The Mist.* Cover and black and white images Dimension Films Blu-Ray, 2007.

PG 12. "Back In Black...and White!" Dave Hinchberger. 2020. Original.

PG 12. Frank Darabont. *The Mist* interview with Frank Darabont. Mist, The. 2007, Dimension Films Blu-Ray.

PG 13. Frank Darabont quote. Kent, Alexandyr. "'A Bad Day at the Market.'" March 23, 2007. *The Times.*

PG 14,15. *The Night Flier.* Japan DVD cover art. Coming soon poster art.

PG 16, 17. "The Rock," Dave Hinchberger. 2020. Original.

PG 18. "Big Driver," Dave Hinchberger. 2020. Original.

PG 18. *Big Driver.* Lifetime Movie poster art, 2014. Lifetime Network.

PG 19. *Big Driver.* Japanese DVD Release artwork.

PG 21. *Die Verurteilten (The Shawshank Redemption).* Warner Home Video, Germany, 2019 DVD.

PG 22. "Mangled, in Name Only," Dave Hinchberger. 2020. Original.

PG 22,23. *The Mangler.* VHS home video cover and tape artwork. 1995 New Line Home Video. Turner Home Entertainment.

PG 22. Nicholas Moreau. *The Mangler.* "Voice Actor Jim Cummings Fills Room At The Fan Expo Canada." diskingdom.com, Sept 2, 2018.

PG 25. *Children of the Corn*, UK VHS cover art, 1984 New World Pictures. 1998 Cinema Club packaging design.

PG 26. Did You Know? *(Dreamcatcher).* Dave Hinchberger. 2020. Original.

PG 26. Regal Cinemas theater tickets, 2003 showing of *Dreamcatcher.*

PG 28. Did You Know? *(Dolores Claiborne).* Dave Hinchberger. 2020. Original.

PG 28 [1]. Neal Conan. "Kathy Bates: Storefront Lawyer On 'Harry's Law'". NPR. January 26, 2011.

PG 28. *Eclipse Total (Dolores Claiborne)* Spanish DVD art. 2000 Warner Bros.

PG 30,31. "Back From the Dead... Again." Dave Hinchberger. 2020. Original.

PG 31. *Pet Sematary*, 2019 UK Movie Poster Art. PG .

PG 33. Canadian American Records, Ltd. Sleepwalk record label. New York, 1959.

PG 33. Dick Clark. Dick Clark's Saturday Night Beechnut Show. August 01, 1959. "Billboard #1 Pop Hits — 1950-1959". Record Research Inc.

PG 34,35. "The Lost Prologue." Dave Hinchberger. 2020. Original.

PG 34. Evil Troll tattoo art by MonsterTattoo on Tumblr.

PG 35. *Cat's Eye* German Blu-Ray, *Katzenauge.* 2017 Koch Media, Germany.

PG 36. "The Sparrows Are Flying..." Dave Hinchberger. 2020. Original.

PG 37. Sophia Waterfield. "What is Triskaidekaphobia and How Do You Pronounce It? Why Those With a Number 13 Phobia Fear Friday the 13th," Newsweek online, 9/13/19

PG 38. "Creepshow 2, Creep-A-Zoids!" Dave Hinchberger. 2020. Original.

PG 38. *Creepshow 2* Waxworks Records, 2017 Vinyl Release. Waxworkrecords.com

PG 40. "Which Is It?" Dave Hinchberger. 2020. Original.

PG 40. George Romero. *Creepshow* Blu-Ray commentary, 2018 Scream Factory.

PG 40. *Tales From the Darkside* Blu-Ray cover art, 2020 Shout Factory. VHS cover art, 1990 Paramount Pictures.

PG 42. "I'll Teach You To Throw Away My Comic Books!" Dave Hinchberger. 2020. Original.

PG 44. The Stanley Hotel. Estes Park, Colorado, USA.

PG 46,47. "Talk About Dull." Dave Hinchberger. 2020. Original.

PG 46. Kubrick, Vivian. Making of "The Shining" 1980 documentary.

PG 47. Christopher Hooton. "Read the Alternative Phrases to..." Independent.co.uk, 11 June 2015.

PG 49. Bernie Wrightson "ghoul" sketch from *Riding the Bullet*, 2010 Lonely Roads Press.

PG 50,51 "Cell Phone Upgrade." Dave Hinchberger. 2020. Original.

PG 50. Steebin1 on YouTube. Stephen King *Under the Dome* Book Signing - Dundalk, Maryland 11/11/09.

PG 52. Did You Know? *(Firestarter).* Dave Hinchberger. 2020. Original.

PG 54. Did You Know? *(1408).* Dave Hinchberger. 2020. Original.

PG 56. Did You Know? (Castle Rock Newsletter / Dolan's Cadillac). Dave Hinchberger. 2020. Original.

PG 56,57. Castlerock logo. Castlerock Newsletter, the newsletter by Stephen King, 1985 to 1989.

PG 57. "A Nod To Poe." Dave Hinchberger. 2020. Original.

PG 58. "Reimagined." Dave Hinchberger. 2020. Original.

PG 58. Justin Froning. *Stand By Me* Movie Poster commissioned art. thehousebear.com

PG 60. Did You Know? *(Maximum Overdrive).* Dave Hinchberger. 2020. Original.

PG 60,61. *Maximum Overdrive* Collector's Series Blu-Ray cover, and truck art. Artisan / Lionsgate, 2018.

PG 60. [1] Tony Magistrale. *Hollywood's Stephen King.* New York: Palgrave Macmillan. p. 20. November 22, 2003

PG 60. [2]. Bob Thomas. "'Selling' his movie is a new chore for author Stephen King". Associated Press. July 23, 1986.

PG 63. Did You Know? *(Pet Sematary).* Dave Hinchberger. 2020. Original.

PG 64-67. "King Goes Into Overdrive." Tyson Blue. 1986 / 2020. Originally appeared in *Twilight Zone*, Feb. 1986.

BIBLIOGRAPHY

PG 64-67. *Maximum Overdrive* photos, 1986 De Laurentiis Entertainment Group.

PG 72, 73. "Is It Hot in Here or is it Me?" Bryan McAllister. 2020. Original.

PG 73. *Cujo* movie cover paperback edition, 1982 / 1983 Signet / New American Library.

PG 74,75. "Danny Cam." Dave Hinchberger. 2020. Original.

PG 74,75. [1]. Nicholas White. "How 'Doctor Sleep' Filmmakers Pulled Off That 'Shining' Cameo," Oct. 30, 2019, Variety.com.

PG 75. Anthony Breznican. "Shades of The Shining: Hunting for Easter Eggs in Doctor Sleep." Vanityfair.com, Nov. 9, 2019.

PG 76. "From Saint to Sinner." Dave Hinchberger. 2020. Original.

PG 76. Allen Koszowski. Artist for *Needful Things* promotional card. Overlook Connection Bookstore. 1988.

PG 76,77. *In Einer Kleinen Stadt*, German *Needful Things* Blu-Ray, Euro-Video. Heston, Fraser. Commentary notes from *Needful Things* Blu-Ray, KL Studio Classics

PG 78. *Graveyard Shift* Cover art for UK VHS release.

PG 79. "The Maine Thing." Dave Hinchberger. 2020. Original.

PG 79. [1]. Mike Fleming Jr., "Stephen King On What Hollywood Owes Authors When Their Books Become Films: Q&A". February 2, 2016. Deadline.com

PG 80,81. Brian Skuttle. "Andy Muschietti's *'IT'*- Friends and Fear." 2020. Original.

PG 81. Stephen King. *IT*, 2017 Scribners hardcover edition.

PG 81. Stephen King *IT* Italian edition cover.

PG 82. *Horrorstory*, a *1408* remake, India, IMDB.com, Wikipedia.com

PG 82. Did You Know? (*1408*, India remake). Dave Hinchberger. 2020. Original.

PG 85. Jared Boyd. "Producer confirms Stephen King film production in Mobile" Oct 18, 2016. AL.com

PG 85. Jack Shepard. "Gerald's Game: How director Mike Flanagan made Stephen King's 'unfilmable book' into a film." 28 September 2017. independent.co.uk

PG 85. *Gerald's Game*. Dave Hinchberger. 2020. Original.

PG 86. Roger Ebert. *Hearts in Atlantis*. September 28, 2001 rogerebert.com.

PG 86,87. "We're all just passing through, Kiddo." Dave Hinchberger. 2020. Original.

PG 87. *Hearts in Atlantis* press photo sheet. Village Roadshow Pictures, Castlerock Entertianment 2001.

PG 88. *Hearts in Atlantis*, Japanese DVD cover art.

PG 89. *Mercy* movie art, Blumhouse Productions, Wonderland Sound and Vision. 2014.

PG 92,93. Bradford Evans. "The Lost Roles of Bill Murray." Splitsider.com, February 17th, 2011.

PG 94. [1]. Douglas Winter. (1985). *Faces of Fear*. New York: Berkley Books. p. 177. ISBN 0-425-07670-9.

PG 94. *Thinner* Japanese DVD cover art.

PG 95. *Thinner* press photo, Tom Holland and Stephen King on the *Thinner* film set. 1996 Spelling Films

PG 97. *Esquire* Magazine cover, 2012 August.

PG 100. Did You Know? *(Carrie)*. Dave Hinchberger. 2020. Original.

PG 100. [1] Jennifer M. Wood. "15 Creepy Facts About Carrie." Oct. 19, 2018. mentalfloss.com.

PG 101. *Carrie* movie logo, MGM DVD.

PG 102,103,104,105. "A Moment on the Mile No. 1: Tom Hanks Bathroom." Dave Hinchberger. 2020. Original

PG 106. "Assembly by Hitchcock." John Carpenter. Commentary. 2004 *Christine* Columbia Pictures DVD Special Edition.

PG 106. "Assembly by Hitchcock." Keith Gordon. Commentary. 2004 *Christine* Columbia Pictures DVD Special Edition.

PG 108. *1922* artwork, 2017 Netflix.com.

PG 109. Did You Know? *(1922)*. Dave Hinchberger. 2020. Original.

PG 109. [1] [2] Jordan Crucchiola. "1922's Thomas Jane on Working With Rats and Raging Against the Machine." 2017, Oct. 31. Vulture.com

PG 110,111. "Apt Pupil – Text to Screamplay!" Dave Hinchberger. 2020. Original.

PG 111 Stanley Wiater; Christopher Golden; Hank Wagner. *The Complete Stephen King Universe*. 2006. Macmillan. p. 330. ISBN 0-312-32490-1. (P. ??, 3)

PG 111. [1] [2] Stephen Schaefer. "Good out of evil: 'Usual Suspects' director brings Stephen King novella to film". October 18, 1998. *Boston Globe*.

PG 111. *Apt Pupil* German Movie Poster, 1998 Sony Pictures Releasing.

PG 112 [1]. Ethan Sacks. "Stephen King spills secrets behind his new creepy film, 'A Good Marriage.'" OCT 01, 2014. nydailynews.com

PG 112 [2]. Annie Martin. "Stephen King details new film 'A Good Marriage'" Sept. 14, 2014. upi.com.

PG 113. "Sleepy Hollows Kingly Visit." Dave Hinchberger. 2020. Original.

PG 113 [1]. Krista Madsen. "Stephen King's 'Good Marriage' Housed in Hollow." Apr 30, 2013. patch.com/new-york/rivertowns

PG 113 [2]. Barbara Livingston Nackman, "Stephen King movic to shoot in fabled Sleepy Hollow." *The (Westchester County, N.Y.) Journal News* May 2, 2013.

PG 114,115. "The Lost Stephen King Film," Dave Hinchberger. Wikipedia.com, IMDB.com

PG 115. *Apt Pupil* Haven Bound edition, Cover art. Limited to 150 copies and signed by artist, Glenn Chadbourne.

PG 116. "Get a Leg Up!" Dave Hinchberger. 2020. Original.

PG 116. Tom Spina. *Misery* leg recreation, tomspinadesigns.com

PG 117. Kathy Bates Academy Awards® acceptance speech for Actress in a Leading Role for *Misery*, March 25, 1991, Oscars.org

PG 117. *Misery* placard from YourProps.com, a museum for movie props and costumes.

PG 117. [2] Nikki Finke. "James Caan Enjoying His 'Misery" Page 2 – *Los Angeles Times*. November 29, 1990.

PG 117. Did You Know? *(Misery)*. Dave Hinchberger. 2020. Original.

PG 117. [1] William Goldman. *Which Lie Did I Tell?: More Adventures in the Screen Trade*, published by Pantheon, 2000. p 42-44

PG 104. *The Green Mile* UK 15th Anniversary Blu-Ray cover art.

Glenn Chadbourne Artwork, copyright 2020. Featured on pages; 3,4,17,24,27,29,30,32,39,41,45,50,51,59,62,63,64,65,66,67, 68,70,71,72,75,76,79,80,87,88,89,93,96,98,102,103,106,118,119,12 0,121,122,123,124

Dedicated to my lovely wife, LeeAnn, a mother, a teacher, who inspires so many.

She's my inspiration, every day.

As she says, "Work smarter, not harder."

Thank you to our contributors for their dedication of the wonderful pieces published within this years edition. A glorious thank you to my long time partner in so many projects, the featured artist within, Glenn Chadbourne. You're a cool ghoul, my friend.

A special thank you to Anthony Northrup who faithfully administers ALL Things King - A Stephen King Fan Page on Facebook and who was a big help with research for this edition.

To our graphic designer, Bryan McAllister, who always delivers beautiful editions for our press. This year's calendar was certainly a challenge, but what a fun ride!

Stephen King Catalog 2021 Desk Calendar:
Stephen King Goes to the Movies

Published © 2020 by Overlook Connection Press PO Box 1934, Hiram, Georgia 30141

OverlookConnection.com StephenKingCatalog.com

First Printing ISBN: 978-1623307004

www.ingramcontent.com/pod-product-compliance
Lightning Source LLC
Chambersburg PA
CBHW081132300726
48982CB00005B/933
* 9 7 8 1 6 2 3 3 0 7 0 0 4 *